SPIRIT
OF THE
WICHITAS

Daphne,

Enjoy!

David R...

SPIRIT
OF THE
WICHITAS

DAVID ROLLINS

TATE PUBLISHING
AND ENTERPRISES, LLC

Spirit of the Wichitas
Copyright © 2016 by David Rollins. All rights reserved.

No part of this publication may be reproduced, stored in a retrieval system or transmitted in any way by any means, electronic, mechanical, photocopy, recording or otherwise without the prior permission of the author except as provided by USA copyright law.

This novel is a work of fiction. Names, descriptions, entities, and incidents included in the story are products of the author's imagination. Any resemblance to actual persons, events, and entities is entirely coincidental.

The opinions expressed by the author are not necessarily those of Tate Publishing, LLC.

Published by Tate Publishing & Enterprises, LLC
127 E. Trade Center Terrace | Mustang, Oklahoma 73064 USA
1.888.361.9473 | www.tatepublishing.com

Tate Publishing is committed to excellence in the publishing industry. The company reflects the philosophy established by the founders, based on Psalm 68:11,
"*The Lord gave the word and great was the company of those who published it.*"

Book design copyright © 2016 by Tate Publishing, LLC. All rights reserved.
Cover design by Jim Villaflores
Interior design by Richell Balansag

Published in the United States of America

ISBN: 978-1-68352-638-4
1. Fiction / Native American & Aboriginal
2. Fiction / Action & Adventure
16.07.04

For Mom, Paul, Susan, and Mark

Acknowledgment

To my family and relatives who inspired this novel: Sharon (Jackson) Rollins, Paul Rollins, Susan (Rollins) Stinson, Mark Rollins, Ralph Lee Jackson Jr., Maria (Reynolds) Jackson, Melissa Jackson, Steve Jackson, and Brian Jackson.

To Bob and Robin Lee for your friendship, historical reference, and inspiration of your southwest Oklahoma ancestry.

To Dorman Chasteen Jr., my third cousin, for your historical reference of our southwest Oklahoma ancestry.

To my southwest Oklahoma ancestry that influenced this novel: John and Minnie May (Harris) Havens (my great-great-grandparents who settled southwest Oklahoma Territory in 1900), John and Verna Viola (Havens) Gossett (my great-grandparents), and Ralph Lee and Nelda Mae (Gossett) Jackson (my grandparents).

To Quinton Smith, Randy Hale, and the staff of the Wichita Mountains Wildlife Refuge for your friendship and historical reference.

To John, Julie, Megan, and Morgan Magness for your friendship and inspiration.

All my love to my wife, Kim, for her patience, love, and understanding of my desire to write. And to my children, Kaitlyn and Nathan, I love you.

Thank you, God, for this wonderful variable in my life.

Prologue

The late December wind churned the hope for snow as it whistled against the nearby window. An old man sat comfortably in a brown vinyl recliner recalling a snowfall on the same night many decades ago. The opened doors of a wood-burning stove presented the warmth of an established fire. The fire reigned as the master display for the entire living room. As the only source of heat except for the rarely used propane, the family instinctively migrated into the room for warmth and nostalgia. The cast-iron burner radiated warm waves that buffered the room from the wintry onslaught. The small pile of split wood next to the hearth dwindled with each passing hour. The pile beckoned the nearest passerby to become the next candidate to brave the blustery cold and restock from the ample stack outside. The old man watched the mound of coals simmer. They transitioned in shades of orange and red, illuminating the dimly lit room in a sunset hue. The flames burned the wood with soothing control as the logs crackled a comforting presence.

The slow fade of small string lights alternated in colors of red, green, orange, and blue. A seven-foot artificial fir tree was located safely away from the fireplace. The festive tree was adorned with brilliant strands of lights, silver and gold garland, and numerous multicolored, chipped glass bulbs that hinted to years of previous use. The tree stood with a sentimental existence alluring anyone entering the room to its seasonal setting. Dark green garland adorned the mantle above the wood stove, resembling lush cedar limbs carefully preserved in a woven pattern. Single electric candles were placed on the lower ledges of the windows. Each candle burned a red candescent bulb for highway passers to observe across the half-acre front yard.

The old man took a beckoning sip of his eggnog. The thick treat represented the taste of the holidays. He rested his head against the recliner, still relishing the beverage. The aroma of the previous thirteen-pound oven-roasted turkey and homemade cornbread dressing lingered. It bowed in turn to the stirred scent of spiced mulberry and cinnamon-stick potpourri simmering on the wood-burning stove. An occasional whiff of warm apple-clove cider with orange slices managed to escape the kitchen and tease the adults into another sampling. The cling of kitchenware and the whine of a blender indicated the progression of homemade hot chocolate and whipped cream. The rich, chocolaty goodness combined with the real whipped cream to create a beverage surpassing any child's expectation.

The old man listened to the record player broadcast the mellow tones of Perry Como throughout the room. The harmonious lyrics of "The Christmas Song" united his soul with the feeling of his favorite holiday tune. Each measure of the song invoked the feeling of Christmas, *his* feeling of Christmas. The personal joy of the wintry festival and its spiritual meaning flowed with his childhood memories. He treasured his rejuvenation and enjoyed another Christmas Eve in Frederick, Oklahoma.

"He looks so happy," a young wife whispered to her husband standing at the living room entry.

"Yes, he does. He really thought 1984 would be his last Christmas."

"I know. But that was last year. And here we are a year later."

"And another year blessed," the husband added.

"You two talked a long time today. Did you get everything you needed from him?"

"Yes. He wanted to finish today. I should be able to complete the chronology next week and then start the narrative. With some effort, I think we will finally have a fully documented family history," the husband stated.

His wife looked at the old man still trained upon the fire. "I hope you can finish it soon. It would be awful if he…"

"I know," the husband said as he held his wife close. "I don't like to think of it either." He glanced at the Christmas tree absorbing the holiday ambiance as "That Christmas Feeling" began to play. He smiled at the appropriate timing of the song and its befitting words that complimented the scene in musical harmony. Pausing to coalesce with the merriment before him, he watched the old man with subtle appreciation. "A Christmas with my grandfather."

His wife kissed him on the cheek as the outside door flung open. The tranquility of the moment was whisked away by the rush of two children. The parents witnessed a bundled eight-year-old girl and a shivering four-year-old boy standing with rosy cheeks and anxious grins.

"Did Sanna Cause come yet?" the little boy yelled with his earmuffs still on.

"Uh," the husband sighed as his wife hurried to close the door and unravel their heavily clothed children.

"No, I told you we have to be asleep," the impatient sister replied.

"You two are frozen," the mother stated as she helped remove their coats and boots. "All right, play time is over. Let's get out of these clothes and into your jammies."

"I'm cold!" the little boy exclaimed and tossed his boot on to the pile of winter wear.

"It's a good thing I have some hot chocolate on the stove," the mother responded.

"Yay!" the children cheered and raced into the kitchen. The father positioned two cups on the table already filled with the steamy beverage. The children sat on the wooden bench seats of the long rectangular table and grasped their cups. They upended the warm drinks without burning their tongues.

"More!" the little boy bellowed with his earmuffs still on.

"Is that how we ask?" the mother questioned.

"Peaz more!" the little boy replied in his pronunciation. The father yanked off the earmuffs and sat next to his children.

"Hey, you two, when you finish your hot chocolate why don't you go into the living room and talk to Great-Grandpa Matthew before you go to bed. I think he would like that."

"Will Sanna Cause come if there's a fire? Will he get burned?" the little boy asked and wiped his chocolate-ringed mouth with his white sleeve.

"No," the father laughed, dabbing his son's face with a napkin. "Santa Claus knows what to do. Come on."

The two children ran into the living room and surrounded the old man. He beamed eagerly at his great-grandchildren. "My! Don't you both look like little icicles coming in to thaw? Hop up here and see me." They climbed into the chair, and he hugged them with a warmth no fire could achieve. "How are my little elves doing?"

"We're not elves! They are loading Sanna's sleigh right now," the little boy said.

"Oh, I guess they are, aren't they?"

"Great-Grandpa Matthew, are you going to stay with us for Christmas tomorrow and see our presents?" the little girl asked.

"I sure am. I have some presents I want to give you and your brother too. In fact, I may just sit right here all night and make sure ole Santa leaves you all the presents he can bring." The little girl smiled and leaned against him.

"You can't sit here all night, you'll burn up!" the little boy exclaimed.

Matthew laughed. "No, this is a nice fire, but I used to sit next to much bigger fires when I was near your age. And most of our fires were outside in the cold."

"Didn't you freeze?" the girl asked.

"Oh, no. We had big fires called bonfires. We would burn them every Christmas Eve outside on our land. We enjoyed our bonfires. It made Christmas very special for us because for many years that was all we had for Christmas."

"Did you have a favorite Christmas, Great-Grandpa? Did Santa bring you lots of toys?"

He remembered an episode from his past, long buried within the recesses of his life. He addressed the eagerness of his great-granddaughter with tears. He hugged her with renewed strength and kissed her on the forehead, hoping to hide his emotion from her curiosity.

"What's wrong with Grandpa Matthew?" the wife whispered to her husband watching from the sofa across the room. The husband observed without reply, waiting to see what the situation would reveal.

"Thank you, little Kaitlyn, and how interesting it is that you would ask that. I actually do have a favorite Christmas. It is one that I have not remembered for a very long time. I was about your age when I had my favorite Christmas."

"Did you get a bike? I wanna tri-bike-cycle for Christmas!" the little boy shouted gleefully. "I'm gonna ride it really fast!"

Matthew rubbed his great-grandson's head. "Nathan, I sure hope Santa brings you that tricycle. I'm sure your mommy and daddy will be quite upset if he doesn't!" Matthew glimpsed at the parents shaking their heads.

"Nathan, be quiet!" Kaitlyn demanded and readdressed Great-Grandpa Matthew. "So, what was your favorite Christmas?"

"Well," Matthew pondered for an abbreviated version and checked the time on the free-standing grandfather clock. "I was eight years old, just like you, Kaitlyn, and me and my two brothers and my sister had just moved to Oklahoma. It was a cold Christmas Eve like this one tonight. And we had all received a present that none of us could ever have imagined receiving."

"Was it a puppy?" Kaitlyn asked.

"No, it was bigger than a puppy."

"I know!" Nathan interjected. "Was it a dinosaur?"

Everyone in the room laughed. "No, it wasn't that big." He looked into their eyes, enjoying the unscripted moment with a love that defined his God-given role as a great-grandfather. He peered at their mother sitting attentively on the sofa. "If your momma doesn't mind, I would like to give my presents to you now."

"Of course you can, Grandpa," she encouraged.

Matthew whispered to the children, "Hop down and look behind my chair." The children scrambled off the seat and ran behind the recliner. Two small, white boxes rested along the wall, tied with red ribbon bows. Fixated with anticipation, the children hurried back to Great-Grandpa Matthew. "Okay, open them up." The children pulled the ribbons and ripped off the box tops. They removed the white paper, revealing a wooden pendant in each box. Each child held their respective gift in front of Great-Grandpa Matthew while the parents watched with paralleled curiosity.

"What are they?" Kaitlyn asked, holding the circular item.

"They are called dream catchers."

"They're what?" Nathan asked.

"You can hang them in your room or near your bed. People use them in lots of places."

"It looks like a spiderweb," Kaitlyn noted.

"I like the feathers," Nathan added.

"It is like a spiderweb. The web is inside the wooden circle. At night when you sleep, your bad dreams get caught in the web and you don't dream them. While the good dreams pass through and follow down the feathers to you."

"That's neat," Kaitlyn said. "So what was it that you got for Christmas that was so big?"

"We got a bison."

"A what?" Nathan asked.

"A bison." Matthew saw the confusion on their faces. "I guess you all call them buffalo."

"Oh, yeah. I know what a buffalo is. We see them when we visit the wildlife refuge at the mountains," Kaitlyn said.

"That's right. That buffalo was our special present. I got these dream catchers with your Great-Aunt Rachel when we were very young. They are very dear to me because they hold a special memory about our family. So, we got to have a special Christmas because of a buffalo and these dream catchers."

"Can we have a buffwoe for Christmas?" Nathan asked.

"I don't think your mother would want a buffalo running around the house Christmas morning. Let's stick to seeing them on the refuge."

Nathan leaned next to Great-Grandpa Matthew. "Sanna Cause has big reindeer that pull his sleigh! They are bigger than your buffwoe."

"Santa does have reindeer and he is going to fly over our house if you two don't get ready for bed," the mother interrupted.

"Aw! But I want to hear about the buffalo," Kaitlyn countered.

"Don't you worry. I'll finish the story with you sometime. You and your brother get to bed before Santa Claus comes!" Matthew teased.

"Tell Great-Grandpa Matthew night-night and thank him for your gifts," the mother stated. Each child kissed a separate cheek as Matthew hugged them. The children scampered toward the bathroom and their toothbrushes, admiring their dream catchers against the mirror. Matthew watched them hurry away and relished the moment. The cycle of life lived on in his great-grandchildren. His spiritual appreciation of experiencing the evening was expressed in his quiet prayer of gratitude.

"What's this memory about the family and some buffalo? Anything we may have missed talking about earlier?" the husband asked and pulled a chair next to Matthew.

"No. You have been very kind to outline our family ancestry," Grandpa Matthew replied. "Many your age don't seem to care about their family lineage, certainly not to capture it in writing or while their older kinfolk are still alive. You now know their names, but you don't know *who* they were or what their story is."

"Okay, what's their story?"

Grandpa Matthew stared into the fire. "It was more like an event in some ways. It made the family what it is and in many ways saved us. I was waiting to tell you. I haven't even told your father. He never seemed as interested as you are about the family history."

"Here," the mother handed the dream catchers to her husband. Each one was the size of his hand. "I thought you might want to see these. The kids are tucked in. You two don't stay up too late. The kids will get us up early in the morning." She kissed her husband and hugged Matthew.

"That sounds like an interesting story. Are you too tired or do you feel like sharing it?" the husband continued and studied the dream catchers.

"You are the provoking one, aren't you?" Matthew joked. "Sharing it is the easy part."

"Why is that?" the husband asked, welcoming another conversation with his grandfather.

Matthew turned from the fire and saw the two dream catchers. He then stared into his grandson's eyes. Seeing his profound interest and genuine curiosity, Matthew pointed toward the mantle. "I was waiting for a good time to present it to you. It looks like now is that time." His grandson followed his beckoning to the mantle. Another white box with a red ribbon bow was hidden behind the garland. The grandson carried the present back to his chair and opened it. A momentary delay highlighted his grandson's enthusiasm as he removed a leather journal from the box. His grandson studied the journal closely. Its uniqueness and age became obvious by his lack of words to describe it.

He opened the journal to the first yellowed page and witnessed the faded writing. "The Dream Catcher," he read aloud. "Is this a story?"

Matthew watched his grandson rise from his fascination over the journal and prepare for a multitude of questions. Before he could ask, Matthew looked at the journal with vivid recollection. "It is a history. That book is an episode of our family's past." Matthew returned his attention to the fire and drifted back in time. "The title says it all. But to this day, no one in the family has been able to explain it."

1

"Mae! Come on. We need to get a goin'. I'm watching birthdays go by out here!"

"Hold your horses, Ralton! I'm not leaving till this letter is done," Mae snapped at her husband as he stood outside of the Lawton post office. She turned toward the counter and addressed the snickering postal clerk. "I'm so sorry. My husband and I got our bid in the Big Pasture. We came from Montague County, Texas, to get our land. He's really excited. Not that I'm not, it's just that I've got to get this letter to my son and daughter back in Montague County so they will know we made it. I'm sure my grandchildren are worried something awful. Are you sure there is not a post office in the Big Pasture area? What with all of the little towns springing up around there? I was certain there would be a post office closer than here."

The postal clerk stared hypnotically at Mae. "Ma'am, we can have your mail on its way with the next run. And besides, without a return address your kinfolk won't be able to reply to you anyway. Here, let's do this." The clerk hurried to appease Mae and discreetly move her along. "Write your name and then write 'Big Pasture, Oklahoma Territory,' and then today's date, May 10, 1907. At least that will give your kinfolk an idea of where you are and when you mailed this." The clerk smiled at Mae and noticed the growing line of customers behind her.

"Oh, I can't believe I'm doing this! Ralton Junior and Ann will be beside themselves." Mae watched Ralton mount the wagon and prepare the horse team. "Ralton, we need an address as soon as we get there. We will need to mail another letter!" She finished addressing the letter and slid it across the counter.

"Very good, ma'am. We'll get this on its way. Is there anything else I can do for you today?" the postal clerk asked.

"Oh, yes." She leaned toward the clerk. "Do you know exactly which way it is to the Big Pasture?"

The clerk pointed at the wall. "There's a map right back there, ma'am. And if that doesn't work, just point your team west and angle 'em slightly to the left. Have a safe journey, ma'am. Next in line, please!"

Mae looked for the map, unable to see it from the line of people. "Where is this map he's talking about?"

"Mae, get out here or so help me, you're walking!"

"Are you sure you know where we're going? That clerk said there's a map in there somewhere," Mae questioned while the post office customers chuckled at her departure. She climbed on to the wooden bench next to Ralton. He lifted the reins and startled the horses to attention. "Did you find a mercantile?" Mae looked along the sides of the wagon. She observed hoes, rakes, their tub, lanterns, axes, sacks of seed, chests of clothes and sacred belongings piled higher than she remembered.

Ralton steered the team onto the road, giving enough room for their lone milking cow and extra horse trailing behind. "Yes. I found all we needed and then some. I got a good deal on lumber and picked up some more canvas. I grabbed another barrel for extra water and met a guy that might be selling a used plow in a week or so. I told you there was opportunity here. We've done it right. And with Fort Sill just north of here you know it's going to have some order. I met a few soldiers from Tennessee. It wasn't that long ago that I could have been posted here."

"Who do you think you are fooling with that kind of gibberish, Ralton Hutch? The Oklahoma Territory wasn't a thought in anyone's imagination when you were in the army," Mae teased.

Waves of dust tossed in the developing wind. The heat of the early spring day began to rise. Mae fanned the dust from her face. She tasted the swirling earth from a passing coach as they trotted through Lawton. Wooden buildings lined the street. The ruts of numerous wagons and buggies lined the dirt road, providing recent evidence of pioneers and settlers before them. The bustling town showed little indication that its beginning was only six years earlier. The previous presence of tents and temporary dwellings appreciated to more permanent structures that outlined the ruggedness of the maturing town.

Ralton guided the team through steady traffi
wheels. They passed the remaining businesses o
"A feller back at the post office said that is the
and fabrics. Do you wanna stop?"

Mae admired the neatly stacked fabrics in.
to, but we need to save what we have for now. 1 ha.
us through."

"Is there anything else we need before we leave town? There won't be much else in the way of a mercantile once we leave Lawton." Mae stared at the buildings and numerous people. The passing glimpse of civilization consumed her. She turned forward to face their westward future with solemn regard. Ralton cracked the reins and the team stiffened their steps in response.

Mae addressed Ralton with trepidation. "Well, I guess this is it, then."

Ralton steadied the team and wrapped his arm around Mae. "Once we pass those remaining buildings up there, we'll be on our way. Don't you fret any. Soon, we will be standing on virgin land ripe for farming. And the best part is it's all ours! No more abiding by another man's allowances. For the first time in our lives, we own our land." Ralton raised his face to the wind, displaying fortitude that beckoned with every turn of the wagon wheels. His quelled excitement emerged. He thought of their proximity to their destination, nearing with every step. He no longer wanted to contain his anxiety. He urged the team with frequent taps of the reins. The thought of their years spent saving money, sacrificing amenities, and days of sweat-soaked manual labor seemed to fade away. The reality of becoming a landowner surpassed all hardship. "Once we break ground, we'll have a harvest compared to no other. You'll see. We'll save just like before and get started on a house and everything we need. We're gonna make it, darlin'!" He kissed Mae on her cheek while they passed the western outskirts of town.

"Oh, I know," Mae responded with hidden resolve. "Lord willing, we'll make it." She looked northward. "Are those the same mountains we saw on the way in?"

"Yep. I think they call those the Wichita Mountains."

"It's hard to believe there are mountains out here on the plains. I hope we have a view of them from our land."

hugged her a second time. He adjusted his hat against the wiped the sweat from his brow. The open prairie beckoned. He ed both reins, overjoyed with the next phase of their life on one .idred and sixty acres of pride and promise. Mae grinned at Ralton's enthusiasm and subtly observed the vastness before them. The land spread toward the blue horizon with the grass tossing in the wind. The passing clouds cast patchy shadows across the ground. The view stretched beyond her comprehension. She raised her head toward the sky, harboring potential tears. Summoning the heavenly realm for a woman's comfort, she closed her eyes in another silent prayer.

The orange light of the campfire flickered against the canvas as Mae watched the spectacle within the wagon. The padded bed comprised of quilts and burlap against the wagon floor provided relief from the dew-covered ground. An opening at the back of the wagon allowed a breathtaking view of the cosmos. Countless stars pierced through the blackness. Mae and Ralton settled for the night in quiet observation. Crickets chirped while a coyote's faint howl echoed across the plains. The flames began to subside as Mae nestled closer to Ralton.

"The fire is burning out," she warned.

Ralton refused to move from his comfy spot on the fabrics. "It will die down a bit, but it won't burn out. That never-ending wind will keep fanning it."

"I hope so."

Ralton rolled onto his opposite side. He glimpsed through the canvas opening at the stars. "Isn't this better than the first time we did this?"

"It certainly has been awhile. Goodness, the last time we slept under the stars was up north, wasn't it?"

"Yep. The land run of '89."

"What was the name of that tent town we stayed in?"

"Norman. I think that's what everyone called it. That was a boomin' place, wasn't it? You couldn't hear yourself think at night," Ralton recalled.

"I didn't like it," Mae added. "There were too many people. And those folks that caused such a mess getting to the claims before everyone else. What were they called?"

"Smart?"

"No, but it did start with an *S*."

Ralton chuckled. "They called them Sooners."

"All of those God-fearing people just trying to get some land. And then they have to run into folks that don't follow the rules. I reckon just calling them *Sooners* is letting them off easy. Lord knows there are more harsh names they could be called. But I guess that doesn't matter now."

"Yeah, I know. We didn't fare too well up there. It wasn't meant to be. But, listen." Ralton moved the canvas opening wider. "Not a sound except for nature itself, quiet and peaceful. The land office got it right this time. We got a fair shot at grabbing the last bit of land open in the territory. And there's no one to take it from us this time. This was meant to be, darlin'!"

"It does seem that way, especially when you compare it to that land run of '89. It's just…" Mae paused.

"What?"

Mae peered out of the wagon. "Everything seems so distant this time. Ever since we left Lawton this morning, it's felt like we're the only ones on the prairie."

"You aren't missing those young'uns down south, are you?"

"I miss them something awful."

"Listen. We'll get to our land and get settled. Once I get a plow and get some ground worked, we'll send word for them to come up early."

Mae rose from the bedding. "Do you mean it?"

"Of course. From the looks of it, I could use their help getting started. Lord knows I'm not getting any younger." Mae embraced Ralton. The couple held each other while the territory wind whisked the remaining flames away, leaving a pile of glistening coals in the Oklahoma night.

The morning sun cast a shimmer across the swaying prairie grasses. The wind blew the vegetation in waves that cascaded ahead of the wagon team. The light peeked over the horizon, providing illumination to their rejuvenated journey. Ralton and Mae bounced along on the wagon seat. The expanse of the Great Plains was rivaled only by the brightening sky. Their early start, energized by anxiety, accumulated precious miles ahead of schedule. Sleep was sacrificed for the motivation of expediency. A hurried breakfast of leftover biscuits, thick-sliced salt pork, and hot coffee fueled their momentum.

Mae watched a scissor-tailed flycatcher swoop into the grass for a morning meal. The cloudless sky and vast plains swept away her doubts. She felt the breeze pass through her hair. She reached for her bonnet and noticed the ground below. "Ralton." She pointed toward the soil.

"Looks like we aren't the only ones out here after all," he stated as they passed over some wagon wheel ruts. "I'm surprised it's taken this long to see signs of other folks. Who knows, maybe we'll have good neighbors."

"I certainly hope so. How wild is this territory?"

"Any wild in this country is long gone. The Indians own a big chunk of land somewhere around here. All the buffalo that they know of are gone. And any outlaws are few and far between. I was talking to the owner of the mercantile and he said everyone here is expecting the Oklahoma Territory to become a state, most likely this year. Once that happens, any wildness will be history."

Mae watched the wind swirl over a dry wash funneling red dirt high into the air. The outline of a vibrant dust devil rushed across the ground. "The wind sure does blow a lot here. And the earth is so red in color. Will it be good for planting?"

"It will be fine," Ralton replied. "Plowing it for the first time will be some work, but I hope we don't have to clear too much. Those mesquites are nearly impossible to uproot."

The day passed with every turn of the wagon wheels. Ralton checked his map, certain they were close to their land. They trotted up a small rise in the terrain. Reaching the top of the ridge, they gasped at the view before them. The land leveled, stretching into the horizon and inhibited only by another tree line in the distance. Ralton stopped the team.

"Do you see that pile of rocks? It looks like someone put them there," Mae questioned.

"Yee-ha! That's using those purty eyes, my darlin'." Ralton jumped from the bench. Mae watched him leap into the air when he observed the rocks. He waved at Mae and ran toward the wagon. Out of breath, Ralton extended his hand. "Would you care to step down from that carriage and join me?"

Mae stared at her giddy husband, perplexed by his unusual behavior. "So what is that pile of rocks?" she asked and offered her hand to Ralton. She landed firmly on the ground, stretching her legs in relief.

"How does it feel to be standing on your own land?"

"We're here? Is this our land?"

"It sure is! There's a marker in that pile of rocks. You happen to be standing in the northeast corner of the finest land God made on earth. And darlin', the best part is it's all ours!"

"We're home," Mae whispered.

"Yes, we are." He looked across the expanse. "We're home."

Ralton paced his single horse across the terrain. Areas of thick prairie grass intermingled with mesquite groves. He dreaded the day when he would have to clear the natural barriers. Pristine woods lined each side of the nearby stream with stands of persimmon, pecan, redbud, and oak trees. Intermittent clearings of dirt mounds and trimmed grass indicated prairie dog towns. Ralton watched the furry creatures scurry about their holes. Several stood on their hind legs and barked their displeasure of his presence. A circling red-tailed hawk quieted their excitement as they ran for the protection of their holes.

He rode to a clearing along the water-carved edge of the stream. The wind tossed the leaves of the cottonwood trees while the sunlight shimmered across their glossy surface. They appeared as triangular, green flags swaying in the breeze. Birds rivaled each other with their signature songs, perched high above. The peace and beauty of the land brought tranquility to his inspection. He looked at the flowing stream, satisfied with the ample water supply. Taking in the view through a farmer's eyes enticed his urgency to clear the land and break sod for a hopeful harvest. The bags of seed back at his wagon beckoned. He rode up a sloping contour and observed the remainder of his property. In the distance, every possession of his existence waited for his return. His horses strolled in happy relief of their harnesses. His milking cow enjoyed substantial helpings of vegetation. A wisp of smoke rose near the wagon. He watched his wife retrieve some cooking items from a chest. Without words, he nodded his head in tranquil thanksgiving. The picturesque dream throughout his life was now a blessed reality.

"What's for dinner?" Ralton asked and dismounted his horse.

Mae wiped her hands across her apron. "We've got some beans and the last of the bread. How was your ride? Did you see the entire property?"

"No, but what I did see sure is beautiful. We have enough timber to start a decent house and a corral. Clearing the land will be a chore, but that's expected. And the water! We won't have to worry about water. From what I can tell, I think right here is as good a place as any to build. It is high ground, not too far from water, and good pasture nearby that I can plow without clearing. I think this is the spot," Ralton announced.

"What's the name of that stream?"

"The land office called it Deep Red Creek. I just hope they labeled it on my map right. When can we eat, I'm starved."

"Here," Mae handed him a wooden spoon. "You got to stretch your legs, now it's my turn. I'm going to fetch some water for coffee."

"No time like the present, darlin'! I'm going to offload that lumber and get started on a dwelling. We still have a few hours before sundown."

Mae huffed at her husband's expected avoidance to help with the meal. She grabbed a bucket and walked to the creek. A multitude of trees lined the embankment, casting a welcoming shade. She stood on the edge of the bank, looking down several feet to the water below. The land appeared to break away. She noticed the sharp angle of the terrain carved from many years of rushing water. She followed the creek to a draw and slid down. The current passed gently as she removed her shoes and walked into the cool stream. She beamed at the refreshing moment. The water turned a brighter red with each step through the saturated earth. The concerns of their new life drifted away with the dancing ripples.

The canopy of rustling leaves accentuated the sound of rushing water. The sun peaked through the barrier and sparkled across the current. Mae raised her leg out of the water, splashing the bank with childlike joy. She wiped the spray from her face and noticed a white feature along the bank. The color contrasted against the red soil. Surrendering to curiosity, she waded toward the water's edge and knelt by the object. Finding a finger grip, she pulled the object from the soil. "Ralton!"

Ralton pulled his shovel from the ground. He raced toward Mae's voice and stopped at the embankment. Between the shrubs he saw his wife standing with her back toward him. "Oh, thank God, Mae. I thought something was wrong!" His attention shifted to Mae's right index finger shoved into the eye socket of a human skull. Ralton bounded down the embankment. He wrapped his arm around her and pulled the skull from her hand. "Are you all right?"

"Look." Mae pointed. Ralton observed several intact bones along the bank. "I think it's an entire body."

"Come on, let's go." Ralton reburied the skull with his shovel.

They walked back to their wagon. "Who do you think it was?" Mae pondered.

"Out here, it could have been anyone. It could have been a cowboy on a drive, a settler, or anyone passing through. You stay away from that part of the creek and don't let it bother you. We've got some work to do before that sun gets any lower. I sure don't want to spend the night in that cramped wagon again."

"Don't worry. I'm not going back there. As soon as you can, you go bury that body in a proper place. I won't stand for that on our land. It is not fittin'."

"I'll get on it first thing," Ralton reassured her.

Mae noticed the progress Ralton made with their rudimentary dwelling. Several large boards protruded from the ground forming the corner of a square. It appeared to be twice the area of their wagon. She observed the bare ground and Ralton's work to ensure a level foundation. She hoped the remaining boards would be enough to avoid a dirt floor.

"It's been awhile since we've slept on the ground," Mae commented.

"It's only for a spell. This will keep the four-legged critters away until I can get a dugout built and some more lumber. I'll get these boards up and then we'll throw that canvas over the top. That should hold us for the time being."

Ralton returned to his digging as Mae checked her cooking. She sniffed the bubbling aroma and stirred the fire. She shifted her eyes toward the creek, regretting her unfortunate discovery.

The descending sun cast its fading colors upon the approaching storm. The ominous clouds rotated above the plains. The wind asserted its intensity with gusts that ripped through the trees. Branches bent to their breaking point as leaves flustered through the rushing air. Scattered rain fell in prelude to the inevitable downpour. Mae looked toward the west as fear meandered through her veins. The darkening sky boasted no concern for her safety as she hurried to secure their belongings.

"Mae, help me tie the canvas to the boards," Ralton shouted. They worked feverishly as the thunderhead approached. Lightning flashed around them with thunder that detonated in response. A corner of the canvas flew out of her hands. The material flapped in the wind as Ralton secured their only means of a roof. "Let's get inside!"

Ralton shoved one of the boards aside and they entered the one-room dwelling. Rain and wind exploited the crevices between the tightly bound boards. They placed their belongings along the walls for reinforcement. Mae stretched another piece of canvas across the dirt floor and listened to the howling wind. The elements bombarded the outside of the boards with a relentless fury. She fashioned a bed of quilts along the driest section of earth as the water trickled in.

"Ouch!" Mae exclaimed as she pulled her finger from the quilt.

"Are you all right?"

"I must have pricked my finger. It hurts!" Mae turned her attention upward. "The canvas!"

Ralton looked at their fabric roof sagging from the gathering rain. "Push up in the middle before it gives way!" They took some shovels and propped up the canvas. The water splashed outside the boards.

Mae watched the water seep between the boards and turn their dirt floor to mud. She held the shovel in the center of the canvas while Ralton made a pole. Her shoulder muscles burned from the steady tension while water dripped in her face. "I don't miss our life in Texas, but I sure do miss our house!" They watched each other's strained emotion as Mae giggled while favoring her finger. Ralton wiped his soaked head and laughed, taking Mae into his arms and wiping the water from her face. He shoved the pole in place and angled it into the direction of the onslaught.

They sat on the quilted bed and leaned against two water barrels. The lightning, thunder, and rain continued. Ralton watched the boards and canvas through the dim lantern light. He expressed fragile encouragement to Mae and pondered their situation for the night ahead. Mae pressed her face against his chest and addressed the Lord in silent desperation.

Sunlight pierced through the openings among the boards. Ralton turned over on the soaked bedding and rubbed his face. He focused upon the damaged walls. The weak structure shifted in the muddy foundation, creating large gaps between the boards. The overhead canvas drooped from the weight of the water. One corner of the canvas tossed in the morning breeze, capturing Ralton's attention to its torn edge.

Ralton struggled to his feet. He watched Mae resting and stepped around her. He slid on his boots and pushed an angled board outward. He leaned to see the entire area saturated from the storm. The red mud stuck tightly as he stepped from the dwelling. He shivered from his damp clothes. The blue sky appeared refreshed from the dust and pollens of the previous day. Ralton observed the failing integrity of the dwelling and then noticed the wagon.

"Oh no!" He stood in despair at the two severed ropes dangling in the wind. Frustration began to swell within him. The frayed ends portrayed proof of the night's costly toll. He walked toward the dwelling and pushed another board out of the way. "Mae! Wake up. Two of the horses got away last night. I'm going to find them. Do you hear me?" Mae moaned and tossed in the quilt. "I'll be back as soon as I can."

Ralton saddled his remaining horse and tracked around the area. The thorough washing by the storm left little evidence to the direction of the missing horses. Assuming they used the path of least resistance, Ralton turned away from the dense foliage and ventured across the open prairie. He rode within proximity of the creek. The steep embankment provided a natural barrier that directed the horses away. The rains swelled the creek several feet, confirming Ralton's assumption.

What started out as an hour of searching became a day without resolve. Ralton journeyed for miles in every direction with no sign of his horses. Anguish filled his heart as he pleaded in prayer to find his team. With the evening sun slipping away, Ralton reluctantly made his way back to camp. He reached the shallow crossing of the Deep Red Creek and splashed to the other side. Recognizing the steep embankment, Ralton steadied his horse for an angled approach.

He observed the tree line for the best route and straightened in his saddle. A massive black object poised silently on the creek bank above him. His horse bellowed its discontent as the object revealed its distinctive contour. Ralton watched the sun's dying rays illuminate the creature in perfect clarity. He stared at the curved horn of a Great Plains bison. The animal faced Ralton. It stood majestically, undisturbed by the impatient horse. It watched Ralton with a curiosity that hinted at its first encounter with a human. Ralton returned the gesture, amazed at its size and stance. Its height appeared nearly equal to his horse with a considerable advantage in weight and strength. Its long beard and thick, brown fur covered its head and spread to the large hump protruding from its back.

The bison appeared content with Ralton. Fulfilled with the intrigue of the moment, it calmly turned away from the embankment. The bison disappeared beyond the slope as Ralton prodded his horse into action. He hurried along the creek, searching for a means up the embankment. Finding a narrow draw, he urged his horse into an unlikely climb. After three boosts from Ralton's heels, the horse bounded up the draw onto the level ground above. Ralton looked for the bison. Trees and shrubs cluttered the rolling landscape while the sun disappeared into the horizon.

He dismounted his horse and walked to the bison's previous location. Ralton glanced at the passing waters below. A complete human skeleton lay exposed along the bank. Its bleached bones cast a glow against the dark red soil. An arm bone angled out of the soft earth appearing to point at him. The washed skull was half buried in the mud with an eye socket directed toward him.

Ssscuff…ssscuff!

Ralton saw the massive bison standing in the darkness near a stand of cottonwoods. Its front hooves tore at the ground, expressing its disagreement with Ralton's proximity. Overwhelmed by the stunning sight thirty feet away, Ralton peered at his horse.

Grruff!

The threatening grunt triggered Ralton's response. He raced for his mount and shoved his foot into the stirrup. The horse dashed between the trees. Refusing to look behind, he noticed the distant outline of his lodge ahead.

"Mae! You aren't going to believe what I saw!" Ralton yelled and approached the dilapidated dwelling. "Mae, where are you?"

"Ral…ton."

Ralton stepped into the abode. He saw Mae prone near the corner. The lantern burned with enough light to distinguish her features. "Oh no, Mae!" He observed the right side of her body severely red and swollen. Her face appeared nearly unrecognizable from inflammation. Ralton took her arm and held the lantern over it. It was twice its size as she grimaced from the movement. "What happened, darlin'?"

Mae breathed with noticeable effort. "My finger. It started in my finger and ran up my arm. I think something bit me."

Ralton checked her hand. Her finger was swollen to the point of rupture. Ralton rubbed his trembling hand across his face. "What can I do for you?" Mae rolled on to her side. Ralton hurried to dry her. He pulled off the damp spread and covered her with the remaining dry quilt. He placed one of the water barrels near her side and urged her to drink. Struggling to contain his panic, Mae begged him not to leave her side. He tended to his ailing wife as the night began its toilsome episode.

The evening sun's rays extended over the drifting clouds. The vibrancy of the day flourished all around. Boisterous activities of the land's occupants began to calm. The shadows of two oak trees lingered along the ground, appearing as protective cloaks guarding their domain. The flickering leaves provided the appearance of sparkles for a heavenly semblance to the moment below.

Ralton stared at the wooden crucifix a final time. His tired eyes filled with tears as he rose from the dirt mound. An anguished prayer went unsaid. He turned toward the ramshackle remains of the failed dwelling. He watched his cow wander on to the prairie without regard. The wagon stayed where he left it, parked near their first campfire. Its contents were still in good order, but no longer of emotional value. He walked toward his horse and swung his leg over the saddle.

"Hello!" a man shouted from the prairie. Ralton turned to see a group of men riding toward him. He composed himself and turned his horse in the direction of the strangers. "Howdy, ole-timer," the lead horseman greeted with a nod of his cowboy hat. "From the looks of it, I'd wager half a herd of buffalo hides that you are settling here, aren't you?"

Ralton wiped his eyes, unable to see the man's shadowed face. "No, not anymore. My wife passed away. It's only me now." He turned and motioned toward her grave.

"It's just you, huh?" The horseman pulled a revolver from his holster and fired two shots into Ralton's back. Ralton collapsed against the ground. The men hitched two of their horses to the wagon and confiscated the boards and remaining livestock. The lead horseman tied Ralton's feet and dragged him into the trees. He released the rope and looked northward, noticing two men approaching on horseback. He cursed himself for firing twice. He hurried to his mount and galloped south with the departing group while a concealed observer watched the scene from the creek bank.

2

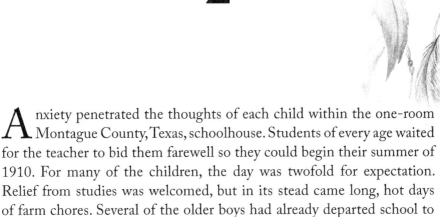

Anxiety penetrated the thoughts of each child within the one-room Montague County, Texas, schoolhouse. Students of every age waited for the teacher to bid them farewell so they could begin their summer of 1910. For many of the children, the day was twofold for expectation. Relief from studies was welcomed, but in its stead came long, hot days of farm chores. Several of the older boys had already departed school to work in the fields or serve as ranch hands. Only the very young knew the meager happiness of summer. And they, too, trained for their future responsibilities on the family farm.

The student on duty rushed outside and pulled the school bell lanyard. The large bell tolled with blissful harmony as the students gathered their belongings. They scattered from the doorway and ran across the countryside toward their homesteads. Three students remained at their desks while the teacher completed the last of her grading. She looked up from her desk and noticed the collective reserve of a nine-year-old boy, a thirteen-year-old girl, and their solemn sixteen-year-old brother.

"Matthew, Rachel, Peter, do you have all of your things?" the teacher asked.

"Yes, ma'am. We're ready," Rachel responded. Her two brothers remained quiet.

"Good. I would feel awful if you forgot something. I need a little more time to finish your grades and then you can be on your way." The teacher paused at their distraught faces. "I am going to miss you three. But, I am sure you will enjoy your new home." She completed her grading and directed the students to her desk. Matthew jumped ahead of his sister.

"Good-bye, Ms. Douglas."

"I'll miss you, Matthew. You're a good boy and a fine student. Keep reading as often as you can." Matthew collected his tablet and ignored his final grade, thinking only of the freedom that awaited him.

Ms. Douglas watched Rachel open her arms. "And I'm going to miss you very much, young lady," Ms. Douglas stated, giving a warm hug. "You take care of yourself, do you hear? And don't give up on your goal to become a teacher. You will make a fine one someday, I just know it."

"I won't give up, Ms. Douglas. Thank you for helping us. I wish I could have known you longer." Rachel began to tear up as Miss Douglas embraced her again. She grinned at the success of her final grade and walked through the door.

Peter remained seated. Taking several seconds, he gradually faced Ms. Douglas. They made eye contact with mutual hesitancy. A presumptuous pause ended with Ms. Douglas sitting next to Peter. "You are more quiet than normal, Peter. What's the matter?"

"Nothing."

"Are you sure."

"Am I going to pass?"

Ms. Douglas handed him his grade.

"Make sure you study more often when you get to your new school. I know you can do it." Miss Douglas watched him remain motionless. "Are you sure you are all right?"

"I don't have a choice, do I?"

"I don't know. Is this about your grade?"

"I was doing fine until…"

Ms. Douglas leaned toward Peter and inquired softly, "Is this about your father again? I know I have only been here a month, but I would like to help if I can."

Peter grabbed his belongings and stood defiantly away from Ms. Douglas. "I hope you like his job. Maybe *you* won't get fired so you can teach longer than a month!"

Peter stared at Ms. Douglas as seconds passed. His emotions churned with strife. With no further words shared between them, Peter stormed out of the room. Ms. Douglas walked to the door and watched Peter lead an angry stride along the dirt road and disappear through the trees.

Rachel and Matthew ran through the woods and across the clearing toward two small houses. Oaks and elms defined a natural separation from the field, which flourished with activity. The children watched two horse teams heave their plows across the terrain. The rugged equipment cut into the earth and folded the rich soil into rows. The teams worked in opposite paths to plow as much as possible with the remaining daylight. The children hid behind the trees waiting for the nearest team to approach. A young man finished a challenging row and turned his horse for another pass. He stopped to wipe his brow as the children pounced from behind.

"Boo!" Matthew yelled.

"Hey! What are you two doing here? Is school out already?" The young man of nineteen years halted his horse and stepped away from the plow. Matthew collided into his brother and wrapped his arms around his dust-covered pants. "Get off me, you little field rat!" Matthew punched his brother and ran for the woods. His brother chased Matthew to the edge of the trees and tackled him in the shade. They rolled along the ground as Rachel stood nearby.

"You look like two pigs fighting over slop," Rachel teased.

Matthew wrestled away from his brother and readied for another charge.

"Whew. Hold on a second, Matthew. I could use a rest."

"I really got you that time, right, Levi?"

Levi chuckled at his youngest brother's enthusiasm. "Maybe a little, but I saw you coming."

"No you didn't! I got you good."

"Have you been plowing all day?" Rachel asked.

"Yep. Me and Uncle Ralton. We've been going since sunup. I'm bushed." Levi looked around. "Where is Peter?"

"I don't know. He left after we did." Rachel replied.

Levi rested his arms across his knees and removed his hat. He watched his uncle start another pass along the opposite side of the field. "It would be nice if he could start another team and help out. What about Samuel and Billy? Did you see them?"

"Nope."

"Boy, the last day of school and your brother and cousins think the work around here has ended too. They had better show up before dark."

Levi dusted off his pants and replaced his hat. "You two get over to the house and see if Maw needs some help loading the wagon. I'm going to do a few more rows and then I'll be along too." Levi rubbed Matthew's hair and hugged him. The youngster grabbed a nearby stick and darted through the trees swinging at each trunk. Rachel remained with her view upon the ground. She kicked the dirt with a reluctant stance that beckoned Levi's attention. "How was your last day of school?"

"Good."

"Did you talk to all of your friends?"

Rachel answered hesitantly. "Yes."

Allowing the moment to mature, he lifted her chin with two fingers. Tears streamed in shallow paths across her cheeks. "What's wrong?"

"They all said good-bye." Rachel buried her head into Levi's chest. Tired from harboring the strain of the day, she released her confined sentiment. Feeling her brother's arms wrap around her, she emptied her sadness with a deep release. Levi rubbed her long, sandy-brunette hair and consoled her without words. The heartfelt scene tugged at him as he fought the developing tears from his sister's anguish. "I don't want to leave."

"I know."

Rachel watched her mother and brother carry various items from the house to the wagon. She thought of their time in the house. It was home to her since birth. The thought of leaving and never seeing her friends again tore at her innocence. "Why did he leave us?"

Determined to remain supportive, he spoke with a soothing reply. "None of us wanted this. I'm sorry about your friends. This is going to be hard, but we have to stick together." Levi struggled for comforting words. His sister's pain was shared within. "It will be all right. Go on to the house and help Maw with the packing. She will be starting supper soon." They embraced each other before Rachel walked away. Levi felt a surge of emotion and clenched his fists. He focused away from his sister's departure and returned to his duties. He provoked the horse into action and drove the plow into the earth, burying his thoughts with every fold.

"Levi!"

Levi saw his uncle approaching across the field. The farm was forged from tall woodlands that bordered around it. Aged oaks and several large elms dominated the established forest. Timber and firewood were plentiful. Every male within the family spent time farming the land in the summers and splitting logs in the forest during the winters. The balance of soil for growing food and wood for shelter and heat provided an immeasurable value for the families. Adjacent to the spread was another field of equal size. An old corn crib faced the second field with a hand-dug well behind it. A trolley fashioned out of a rope and bucket lowered to the only means of water from the distant houses.

The farm appeared as any other in the area except for one original feature. A circular cemetery was enshrined near the center of the first field. Several family members and unknown acquaintances lay in unmarked sites throughout the graveyard. The few headstones that afforded engravings signified servants of the Civil War. Younger trees and saplings grew between the graves, casting a solemn shadow upon the resting. Levi neared the cemetery and contemplated his domestic turmoil. What was once alive and thriving was now a living death. The decision of one entombed his fractured family in a struggle to simply endure. Any hope for tomorrow was buried in a lifeless reality. He observed the graves and thought of those that went before him. The solitude of their remains compared to the emptiness of his presence as he addressed his relative.

"What's the matter, Uncle?"

"That blasted setting sun is the matter!" Ralton Jr. wiped his face.

"We turned a lot of ground today. Good thing you got that new plow."

"Wasn't me. The landowner brought it by. Crop sharing at its finest," Uncle Ralton jeered. "I'm guessing the children are out of school?"

"They got home a while ago. I sent the youngest ones to help Maw load the wagon. I haven't seen Peter or the cousins."

"I will consider them as well rested come tomorrow. I'll work their hides to make up for the lost time today." Uncle Ralton focused upon Levi. "I sure do appreciate your helping out around here. I know you had other things you wanted to do, but you have been a big help. This doesn't put money in your pocket, but it will keep food on the table."

"I needed to help. Besides, I'm not so sure I am cut out to be a ranch hand. Most of my friends already took those jobs. And after what has happened to the family, I figured I best be helping out around here more."

Uncle Ralton cleared his throat. "Yeah. Your maw is still planning to leave. I wish she would think about this. She has no business trottin' off across the plains with those children. She is going to find out quickly what can happen out there without a man to…" Uncle Ralton paused at the realization of his words. He looked at Levi regretfully, unsure of how to continue.

"I know, Uncle. That's why I have decided to go with them."

"You have? What about your…?"

"That doesn't matter now," Levi interrupted. "I have thought about it. I can't leave my family. Just the thought of not being there for Rachel and Matthew is unbearable. I could not live with myself if something happened to them. And I'm not ready to leave Maw either."

"What about Peter?"

"Peter has his own path like anybody. He is coming with us, but I don't know what he plans to do. We have all been dealing with this in our own ways."

"Well, I reckon you best be getting up to the house and helping your maw. I'll get Samuel and Billy to pick up where you left off. Just leave the horse and plow there."

"Thanks, Uncle. Sorry to leave you like this."

"No, you're right. You need to be there for your family. Go on. She will need your help with the heavy stuff."

Levi and Uncle Ralton made brief eye contact and parted with a casual nod. Levi watched his uncle stroll back to his plow horse at a slower pace. Distressed at his lack of parting words, Levi glanced at the cemetery. He sneered at the graves as he started toward the house.

Rachel and Matthew set the oversized chest on the edge of the wagon. Rachel yelled at Matthew to push. The chest teetered on the tailgate and slid toward them. "Watch out, Matthew!"

"I've got it," Levi said and braced the chest. He shoved the chest between two more at the front of the wagon. "Why are you loading those heavy chests? It will take weeks to get there hauling these."

"Maw said to do it," Matthew stated. "She's got two more and we're done. I want to go play."

Levi grinned at his brother. "You go have fun. You too, Rachel. I'll finish helping Maw." The children raced toward their cousins' house.

Levi observed the burdened wagon and walked into the house. The small dwelling had sheltered the family since their arrival several years earlier. The open floor allowed room for a table and five chairs away from the stone fireplace. A rocking chair and two benches decorated the remaining living area. An oversized tub and four feet of wooden counter space designated the kitchen. Handmade cupboards bearing a depleted bag of coffee and a jar of dried beans adorned the tiny enclosure. Years of harvest savings and odd farm jobs from around the area financed the loft above the single bedroom. The family's four children lived snugly in the elevated room. The meager stages of expansion indicated the limited years of provision. He smelled the dusty remnants of the residence. The vague echo throughout the room signified the recent emptiness. Bare walls and a drapeless window were all that remained from the family's occupancy.

"Did you finish plowing?"

Levi saw his mother standing in the door. Loose strands dangled from her failing hair bun as she dabbed her glistening cheeks. "I wanted to help you load the wagon," Levi responded.

"I can get that. You should be helping Ralton get that field ready."

Levi stepped in front of Ann. "I'm going with you."

"Oh. What about your plans?"

Levi grabbed the last chest and carried it toward the wagon. "They can wait."

"Son, I want you to do what you want to do. You are nineteen. Most of your friends have gone."

"I know, Maw." Levi faced her. "I still have time to do what I want." He looked into the wagon. "This wagon is too heavy. We will never get through water crossings with this load."

Ann observed her son's delicate change of topic and placed her hand on his arm. She remained for a moment and then walked toward the house. Levi watched her depart and began shifting the items within the wagon. "I figured it would be too heavy. I didn't want to part with so many of our family belongings," Ann replied by the door. "Unload what you must. We can always come back someday and get whatever is left behind." Ann became quiet and continued into the empty dwelling.

Levi felt the pain of his mother's silence. Anger began to rise within him. He confronted his mother's anguish and his own grief of the situation. He pulled the chests from the wagon and sorted each one to reduce weight. He flung an iron skillet out of the chest, narrowly missing Peter's shins.

"Why don't you watch what you're doing!" Peter yelled.

Levi was startled at the appearance of his brother. "Why don't you get out of the way!"

"Shut up. Does Maw know you are doing this to her things?"

"I see you were able to miss helping out with the plowing again. We can always count on you to duck out of work around here."

Peter tightened his fist. "I ought to punch you in the mouth right now!"

"It will be the last stupid thing you'll ever do," Levi threatened.

"Boys! That's enough," Ann screamed from the house. "Peter, come in here and tell me about school."

Peter glared at Levi. "Good thing Maw saved you from a beat'n."

"Ha! You go on inside to mother while the real men get the chores done. Maybe you can pick a fight with her too."

"I hate you!"

"Do you think I care?" Levi continued his work. Peter rushed at him, slamming Levi against the wagon. Peter pinned Levi against the railing and swung his fist into Levi's back. He unleashed a barrage of hits against Levi, fueled with an inner rage that stemmed from harbored agony.

"I bet you care now!" Peter countered and punched Levi in the head. Levi ducked as Peter swung again, missing his brother entirely. Levi buried his knuckles into Peter's nose. Peter fell to the ground while Levi dove on top of him. He pressed his hand against Peter's face, shoving him into the dust.

"I am sick of you! I ought to break your worthless neck!" Fury filled Levi as he struggled to breathe. He felt his chest surge for air as his breathing rapidly increased. Unable to stay on top of Peter, Levi fell to the side and hyperventilated. Peter scrambled to his feet and watched his brother gasp for air. Unsure of what to do, he backed away from Levi. His breathing began to steady.

"Are you all right?" Peter asked, rubbing his nose.

Levi held his chest. "It doesn't have to be this way." The brothers observed each other in silence and dusted off. Peter sneered and went into the house. Levi walked to the chest and flung it onto the wagon. He climbed in and kicked a chest into place. The top dislodged, sending a leather-bound book flying across the wagon. Levi grabbed the book and threw it back into the chest. The book opened to the first page. He stared at two scribbled words. "*My Journey*," he read. He smirked at the writing. "Yep, all blank after that. How befitting." He pitched the book toward the rear and finished arranging the wagon.

"How was school?" Ann asked Peter.

"It's over."

"You know what I mean."

"I passed."

"Good. I know you did your best. Now, what's got you all upset?"

Peter faced his mother with stern reservation, but loved how she could detect his subtle hints. "Nothing. Why do you want to move?"

"You know why." Ann showed Peter the old letter from his grandparents. "Maw-Maw and Paw-Paw are ready for us. It's been nearly three years. They haven't written in a long time, but we have waited long enough. Oklahoma will be a new beginning for us. We can be a family again."

"No we can't. Paw is gone."

"What I meant was we can be a family with your Maw-Maw and Paw-Paw."

"That's not family, they're grandparents. You can't have a family without a paw!"

"We don't have much of a choice, now, do we?" Ann's lip began to quiver.

"I don't want to go to Oklahoma. I want to go with Paw. I don't want to do any of this!"

"Your paw left, Peter. I don't know where he went. He left all of us."

"Yeah, he probably went someplace better. How do you know he isn't going to come back and…" Peter hesitated as he noticed Levi standing in the door. Peter glared at his brother and stomped out of the room. Levi watched him storm through the woods out of sight.

"I'm sure he's not going to help with the plowing. That would require work," Levi complained.

"Leave your brother alone. Can't you see he's hurting?"

"We all are, Maw. But we still do our part around here."

"He is doing what he can right now, Levi. This is his way of dealing with your father leaving."

"I'm sorry, Maw. I didn't mean to hurt you." Ann acknowledged him with a nod and continued her packing. Disappointed in his behavior, Levi held his arm out in front of her. "I found this in one of the chests. Is it yours?"

Ann wiped her cheek and observed the leather book. "No. This is your grandmother's. She got that a long time ago. She wanted to write about her journey to Oklahoma. It was going to be her journal. She forgot it."

"I'll put it back."

"No," Ann responded. "You keep it. She would want you to have it. It's only fitting. Maybe it will remind you of your plans, your dream." She faced her oldest son. "This is your life. Don't let anyone take your dream from you."

Levi observed the leather cover of the journal and turned to the first page. "Maw-Maw wanted to start her journey."

"Yes. Now it's your turn." Ann grabbed the last of the items and stood quietly observing the empty dwelling. She touched Levi's arm and walked to the wagon.

"Annie, we need to talk." Ann saw her brother Ralton Jr. leaning against the wagon.

"We have talked several times. I am not changing my mind."

"Land's sakes, woman! I just saw Peter running across the field in a fit of anger. This is no good for any of you. Why can't you see that? Wait for the harvest and then we can all go together. It would only take…"

"No!" Ann screamed and threw her belongings into the wagon. She rushed near Ralton Jr., stopping within inches of his face. "Why can't *you* see, Ralton? You want me to stay? Why can't *you* see that it is taking all that I have to stand here and look at this house! I don't want to be here for the harvest. I don't want to be here another day!"

Ralton Jr. prepared for a defiant rebuttal as his wife approached. "Ann, is there anything I can do?"

"No, thank you, Christina. I need to clean the wagon." Ann reached into a chest and pulled out a letter. "Here." She handed the letter to Ralton Jr. "Read this again. Maw and Paw wanted to make the journey. That letter proves they are there. They wanted a new life and so do I."

Ralton Jr. looked at the letter addressed from Big Pasture, Oklahoma. He rubbed his finger over his mother's writing with fondness. He folded the letter and handed it to Ann. His temper subsided at Christina's calming touch.

"I've got some stew simmering. You all come have supper." Christina squeezed Ralton's arm bidding his departure.

"Thank you, Christina. That would be nice. I know the children are hungry. I've had to save money and haven't been able to buy much…"

Christina moved to Ann's side. "Come. I'll round up the children and we'll have a warm meal." Ann wiped her cheek. Christina consoled her sister-in-law and whispered, "Save those tears. Save them for the journey."

The fire ravaged the logs, radiating its warmth from the hearth. The flickering brightness provided the only light in the small living area. Ralton Hutch Jr. rocked slowly with his eyes upon the flames. Christina Hutch and Ann Rowe sat farther away from the fire. The silent tension continued as two pair of eyes peeked from the loft.

"They haven't said a word since supper," a young lady whispered from behind the loft railing.

"I'll be surprised if they say anything," Levi answered his cousin and crawled from his bedding. "That was some argument my maw and your paw got into. I hate to see them fight like that."

"I know. Everything is so different now. I mean, since your, well, you know."

"It's all right, Millie. I know what you mean. His leaving has affected a lot of things."

Millie looked behind Levi at the children scattered across the loft. Her two brothers slept in their single beds with her three cousins nestled upon their sleeping mats. "Do you think your brothers and sister heard them arguing?"

"It doesn't matter. They have all been through a lot. I don't like to see maw and your paw so upset. I don't understand it. You all will be leaving for Oklahoma next year anyway."

Millie continued whispering. "I don't want to go to Oklahoma. My home is here. I think Paw wanted our grandparents to stay. Ever since he got out of the army, he wanted to have his own farm. He doesn't want to leave it."

"But that's the reason for all of this, Millie!" Levi raised his voice. "This isn't his farm. None of us own this land or the houses. That's why Maw-Maw and Paw-Paw left. They wanted their own land for all of us."

"All right, you two," Ralton Jr. interrupted from below. "Millie, roll over and get to sleep! Levi, since you have some steam left, come down here." Levi hurried down the ladder. Ralton Jr. rose from his rocking chair and glimpsed at his sister sitting next to Christina. Ralton Jr. walked to the corner of the room and reached into the darkness. He cradled a rifle and approached Levi. "I developed a liking for rifles when I was in the army. Here, this is a Winchester 94. It shoots true and can hold up to anything." He returned to his rocking chair. "If your maw allows, you can take it with you."

Levi held the hunting rifle with admiration. The sleek barrel connected to the lever action and the contoured wooden stock. The weapon provided a sense of strength. He faced his mother for her approval. Ann stared at the rifle with apprehension and nodded her acceptance. Levi witnessed his mother's reservation and continued studying the rifle. "Thank you, Uncle. It's amazing."

"No," Ralton Jr. interrupted. "It's *everything* when it comes to shooting game for dinner or, God forbid, your family's safety."

"Did you kill anyone with it while you were in the army?" Levi felt the words spill from his mouth with unchecked scrutiny. A momentary silence settled throughout the room.

"I hunted deer with it. I didn't use that rifle in the army. Go put it in a safe place and get on to bed."

Levi blushed and placed the rifle above the cupboard. He climbed the ladder and felt a tug on his foot. He looked down to see his uncle on the bottom rung. "That's a question for when the women are not around," he whispered.

"Thanks again, Uncle." Levi crawled to his mat and ignored Millie's curious stare. He pulled the covers and rolled to his side. The feel of the rifle lingered in his hands. The gift of the weapon further accentuated his respect for Ralton Jr. Levi rarely had discussions of family with his uncle, but he knew of the boldness Ralton Jr. possessed for living. His many years as a cavalry officer chiseled his perspective and hardened him for the bombardments of life. Ralton Jr. loved his family and kept them close. The combination of Christina's Spanish strength and his time-tested endurance made for a formidable, loving marriage. But above all, for Levi, he admired his uncle for fulfilling the titles of husband and father and staying with his family.

3

The rising heat of the summer afternoon invoked apprehension. The dust churned behind the wagon as it rolled along the dirt road. The ruts from previous travelers prevented any hope of a smooth ride. The wagon tossed from the wheels negotiating the bumpy path. The air was calm and dry. The dust seemed to stagnate in the covered wagon, causing the children to cough. The family's third day northward began to test their resolve.

"I knew we should have carried an extra water barrel. The horses will need it," Peter commented from the back of the wagon. Levi ignored his brother's statement, having discussed the topic several hours earlier. He continued driving the horses.

"Why is it so hard for you and your brother to get along?" Ann asked, seated next to him.

"I'm not getting into another fight with him. We talked about that water barrel a dozen times before we left. There is no room. He knows that. He's just picking another fight."

"I wish you two were better toward each other."

"That road runs both ways, Maw. I've tried with him."

"We don't need to give up on each other now." Ann leaned against the wooden bench. The dust from the horses swirled into her mouth while she covered her face.

Levi had changed the subject. "I'm glad you and Uncle got along before we left. I'm sure it meant a lot to him."

"My brother has good intention. But I needed to get out of there. We all did."

"I know. I think the children will see it in time, especially when they get around Maw-Maw and Paw-Paw again. They will help them a lot," Levi paused. "They will help me too."

"I know this is not what you had planned, son. You put your endeavors on hold. But, I am glad you are with us. Your brothers and sister are too."

Levi reached for his mother's hand. "We'll get through this."

"I hope there will be some options for you when we get there."

Levi tightened the reins. "We'll see. Not much has gone to plan for any of us." He smiled at Ann. "And speaking of getting there…" He yelled into the wagon, "You all come look ahead."

Rachel and Matthew scurried to the front while Peter watched from behind. "Oh no! Not another river. We nearly drown crossing the last one," Matthew stated.

"Quit your fussin'," Rachel said. "Now's our chance to get some water and wash up, right, Levi?"

"That's right. But that's not just another river. That's the Red River. Do you see that ridge on the other side? That's Oklahoma."

"We made it?" Matthew asked.

"Yep. But we still have a ways to go yet once we cross. You two get the water barrels ready and we'll stop on the other side."

"Is the water deep?" Rachel inquired.

"It doesn't look too deep. Go ahead. You can lower the back gate." Rachel rushed passed Matthew and Peter and unhooked the gate. She kicked off her shoes and sat on the edge of the wagon. "You all hold on!" Levi warned and steered the team into the river.

Rachel watched the river swell toward the wagon. She dragged her feet in the cool water as they passed through the current. "I see why they call it the Red River," she exclaimed. Matthew and Peter peered out of the wagon. Matthew ripped his shoes off and joined his sister. The water and saturated soil mixed in a rust color from the turning wheels. The river churned gingerly around the wagon. Matthew scowled at the water and struggled to reach it with his foot. Without warning, the wagon dipped along the opposite bank. A sudden splash excited the onlookers, soaking them from the waist down.

The children giggled. Levi halted the wagon on dry land. Everyone hurried toward the river's edge. The children played in the water. Ann refreshed herself with gentle splashes across her face. Levi and Peter unbridled the horses and led them to a welcomed drink. Levi stretched and observed each family member's joy of the moment. "Welcome to Oklahoma!"

"Yay!" the children cheered.

Ann approached Levi and Peter. "I think we could use an extra rest today, boys. Let's set up camp here tonight and let the children relax in the water. It will be a nice break from this heat." Ann retrieved her cookware while Levi and Peter hurried to join Rachel and Matthew. She set a small chest on the ground and looked across the river at Texas. She thought of the journey they had completed and the history they were leaving. Behind them was a life left in ruin, with the promises of love, happiness, and marriage broken by the choice of her ex-husband. She looked at the dirt across her skirt. The red soil caked upon her shoes as she stared again at the distant bank. A smile appeared upon her face. A different land was now beneath her feet. She turned northward at the new life that awaited. *Thank you, Lord*, she thought. *Thank you for our new beginning.* She finished her prayer and ran toward her children. "It's my turn!" she yelled and jumped into the water, shoes and all. She enjoyed the surprise upon her children's faces and exchanged splashes. The steady current washed away the Texas dirt and bathed her in the red earth of Oklahoma.

"Over there! I see smoke rising by those trees," Peter shouted from the ridge.

"Do you think it could be them?" Ann asked, sitting on the wagon bench next to Levi.

"I don't know. It's been nearly a week since we left Lawton, and either that map or the Land Office is wrong. I don't know where Maw-Maw and Paw-Paw are. It all looks the same," Levi replied and steered the horses toward Peter.

"Son, there is nothing wrong with admitting we are lost."

"We're not lost. We're just narrowing it down."

Ann noticed the grin on Levi's face. "Then we'll have half of the Southwest explored by the time we find them." They laughed in spite of their frustrations.

"It's right over there. I saw a few on horseback going in that direction too." Peter pointed ahead.

"Let's hope it's them," Levi responded and snapped the reins. The horse team galloped steadily over the rise. The scenic view opened before them. Cleared land stretched for miles. A small house, corral, and barn accentuated the picturesque view. The structures nestled peacefully along the opposite side of the field. The smoke billowed from a rock chimney at the side of the house. The dwelling appeared large enough to house a few families. Levi noticed two wagons and several horses tied in front. "Something's going on over there. Surely someone can give us better directions."

Levi stopped the wagon near the house. Ann knocked softly on the wooden door and admired the dwelling. The many days of travel created a fondness for four walls and a roof. The door moved slightly allowing a small gap for observation. Suddenly, the door whisked open revealing a blond-haired woman with a wide smile.

"Oh my, new faces! And from the looks of those faces I would say they're tired homesteaders?"

Ann sighed in relief at the cheerful welcome. "Yes, ma'am. You most certainly can say that. I am sorry to interrupt. I am Ann Rowe and these are my children. We have been looking for my parents' land. They got it in the land lottery back in '07 and we can't find them. We've looked all over. I was wondering if you might know of the settlers around here."

"I'm sure I could find out for you." The woman observed the family in detail. "My goodness, you all look exhausted! Please, come in. We are having church service, with it being Sunday. We don't have a worship house so we meet here at my home. It's my family and a few folks from around the area. We would be happy for you to join us. We have a fine meal together afterward. One of the families slaughtered a cow and we are sharing portions. There is plenty." The woman peeked into the house. "They are about to finish the prayer. Ah, where are my manners! My name is Beth, Beth Samson. And who are these adorable children?"

"This is Peter; my daughter, Rachel; my youngest, Matthew; and my oldest, Levi."

Beth looked at the wagon. "Is your husband tying up the team?"

"No, ma'am, this is the Rowe family."

"Lord Almighty! Where have you traveled from?" Beth exclaimed.

"Montague County, Texas. We saw to it that the horses kept a restful pace," Ann joshed.

"My goodness, Ann. You are obviously a strong woman to be braving Oklahoma on your own. Come on in." Beth ushered Ann and the children into the house. The large living area seated several people with their heads bowed. Ann motioned for the children to keep quiet. A large man stood in front of the gathering with his hands clasped.

"Give us strength, Lord, and thank you for our homes and land. Bless us with a bountiful harvest to come, frequent rains and a healthy herd. Amen." The man raised his head and saw Beth. "It looks like you found some new friends. Folks, welcome! Let's find you a seat and get to know you." The large man approached Ann. "Howdy, ma'am. I'm Buck Samson. I'm the proprietor of these parts and husband to this wonderful lady. These are our boys…Boys, stand up!" Two boys rose and acknowledged the Rowe family. "The oldest is Logan and the next one is Daniel. Looks like you have yourself a herd of your own, ma'am." Ann introduced her children as Buck shook hands with each child. He approached Matthew and kneeled. "What do we have here? You look like a scrappy cowhand. I bet you could wrestle a calf to the ground with no problem. Do you like cows, young man?"

Matthew beamed in delight. "Yes, sir. You sure do got big shoulders."

"Well, thank you, little man. I guess that comes from herding cattle all day long. You look rather stout yourself."

Buck and Beth continued the introductions and started the meal. Everyone enjoyed the Rowe family and shared time as though they had known each other for years. Each family spent an hour getting acquainted and learning about each other's history. The blessing of good people and the fortune of worship, food, and fellowship warmed Ann's heart. She watched her children take a rapid liking to Buck and Beth. Levi and Peter realized they had nearly identical ages to Logan and Daniel. Levi finished a second plate of beans and cornbread and talked with Logan.

"Sounds like your family has been here a long time," Levi said.

"We were one of the first to settle the Big Pasture when they opened it. Pop couldn't wait to get his own land and start a herd. Cattle have been in our family for generations. All of the Samsons are cowboys. What do you folks do?"

"Farming, mostly. We never had the money to get into cattle. We had some chickens and a milking cow, but that was about it. My grandfather came up here to get some land and farm. All he talked about was owning his land and farming."

"And you say he settled some acreage around here?" Logan asked.

"I thought so. We've been looking for days now. He and my grandmother came here about three years ago. They sent us a letter saying they made it. So my maw wanted to get here and settle."

Logan chewed slowly on the last of his beef. "You say you had a grandmother?"

Levi paused. "No, I *have* a grandmother." Logan stopped chewing. Levi noticed his sudden expression. "What?"

"Hey, Pop! Can you come over here, please," Logan shouted over the conversations.

Buck noticed his son's appearance. "What is it? You look like you saw a ghost."

"Pop, Levi said his grandparents are the ones that settled that land next to us," Logan stated.

"No, I said they settled somewhere around here. We are not sure where," Levi corrected.

Logan continued with a cautious tone. "He said their names are Ralton and Mae Hutch."

Buck's smile disappeared. Levi detected uncertainty. Buck waved at Beth and motioned for her to bring Ann. The two women approached while Buck escorted the group outside and continued the conversation.

"Yes, my parents are Ralton and Mae Hutch. Oh, this is wonderful! You've met them?" Ann inquired.

Buck watched Beth cover her mouth. He took Ann's hand and whispered reluctantly, "Ma'am, I am so sorry. But your parents passed away nearly three years ago."

Hours passed with Ann remaining in place. Headstones marked two settled dirt mounds. Etchings of *Ralton Hutch* and *Mae Hutch* were barely visible on the rocks. She stared at the graves without words to express. Her eyes were red from crying that had subsided in the first hour. Shock and disbelief soon led to anguish. Sadness transitioned in to a creeping fear of reality. Concern for the unknown became overwhelming. She pondered her present situation and stood between the graves. Whispering a fragile good-bye, she touched the headstones and faced the audience behind her. The children and the Samson family waited for her by the wagons.

"Honey, let's get you home. You need to rest," Beth urged to Ann.

"Home? I don't have a home. My children don't have a home. We have nothing. I don't even know where I am!" She shouted with all of her might. Rachel and Matthew began to cry. Levi consoled them as Peter stood silently. Ann burst into a violent sobbing while Beth yearned to comfort her.

"Ann, you do have a home. It is with us. Come now. It is getting late. We need to bed the children down." Buck motioned her to the wagon.

"I don't have anything, Mr. Samson. My parents were my only hope. I don't have a place to live and I don't have any money. I have nothing!" Ann bellowed.

"Ann, this is a time for prayer. Think of your children. Come get into the wagon." Buck assisted Ann with Beth by her side. Rachel and Matthew walked away.

"Peter, let's go." Peter remained a few yards from the graves, ignoring Levi's call. The silence thickened as Peter's lip began to tremble.

Buck approached Peter and wrapped his arm around him. "Come on, son."

"I'm not your son." He pulled away from Buck and walked to the wagon.

"You can ride with the Samson boys if you want to," Levi offered.

"Shut up. I can ride where I want," Peter countered and sat on the back gate.

Levi shook his head and focused upon Rachel and Matthew. "Come on, you two. It's time to go." Levi watched his sister and brother stand near the edge of the creek. He stared in confusion at the sound of laughter echoing from them. "Rachel, Matthew, let's go!" The two children giggled and waved toward the trees. "Are you two having a good time?" Levi asked.

"We wanted to see the creek. It sure looks deep. All the water around here is red," Matthew exclaimed and sat next to Levi.

"The dirt around here is red, mostly," Levi responded.

Rachel sat next to Matthew. "Levi, are there many Indians around here?"

"What?" Levi started the horse team forward.

"Are there a lot of Indians in Oklahoma?"

"I guess so. Why are you asking that?"

Matthew pushed his sister and fought for sitting space. "Just wondering," Rachel replied, nudging Matthew away from her.

Logan ran from the lead wagon. "Levi, my pop wants you to ride with him. I'll drive your wagon."

Levi jumped from the wagon and warned Rachel and Matthew to behave. He glanced at the back to see Beth seated with her arms around Ann. Peter remained on the lowered gate away from the passengers. A piercing whistle and a crack of the reins put the wagons in motion for the Samson ranch.

"How old are you, Levi?" Buck asked.

"Nineteen, sir."

"Where's your paw?"

Levi dreaded the anticipated conversation. "He's gone, sir. He left us."

"Are you the oldest?"

"Yes, sir."

"Do you think your maw will want to go back to Texas?"

"I don't know. I doubt it. But, like she said, we don't have anywhere to go now."

"Look, son. I didn't want to say this in front of your maw, yet. But your grandpa was murdered. My boys found him nearly dead by your grandma's grave. He was shot."

Levi was stunned. "Who shot him?"

"We don't know. Whoever it was must have been a thief. They took your grandpa's belongings. I had heard of thievery going on around here at that time. But I didn't know it was that bad. I'm truly sorry."

"Yeah, me too."

"There isn't much law around here. A sheriff, I mean. Except for what my boys saw, we don't know much else. They weren't with him very long before he died. I thought it fitting to bury him next to his wife."

"Yes, sir. Seems only fitting." Levi writhed in the conversation.

"Listen. We have plenty of room in the house to bed down your maw and younger siblings. But if you and your brother, Peter, want a bed, I can offer you both a stay with my two cowhands near the barn. I have a small cabin on the side of it. It can house four men in separate beds. It's no hotel stay, but you can get a good night's rest."

"I'm much obliged."

"Good. We'll get you rested and then talk some more in the morning. I'll tell your maw about your grandpa's death. It will be more appropriate if I tell her."

"Thank you. I wouldn't know where to start."

They approached the Samson ranch and stopped near the barn. Beth escorted Ann and the children into the house while Levi and Peter gathered their belongings. Buck opened the cabin door. The remaining daylight complimented two lamps burning near the occupied bunks. The musty smell of dust and sweat provoked a cough from Peter.

"The beds could probably use a good cleaning, but they're softer than the floor. You two can claim what you like. My cowhands ought to be coming in soon. They might take a while to get used to, but they're good men. Drop your loads on a bed and let's get to the house for supper."

Levi tossed his mat, bedding, and a change of clothes onto the bed near the window. "Aren't you coming?" he asked Peter.

Peter sat on the bunk and stared out of the window. "I'm not hungry. I'll put the team in the barn."

Levi observed his brother for a moment and then walked out of the cabin after Buck. Buck walked with the muscled swagger of a seasoned cowboy. His broad shoulders and powerful back fit tightly in his flannel shirt, a testament to working on a ranch. His weathered cowboy hat fit snuggly on his bald head, positioned perfectly to shield the sun at any angle. Levi determined the size of Buck's forearms to be nearly the same width as Levi's legs. His first impression of Buck displayed a man honed by hard work and determination, but approachable and kind. During the ride to the gravesites, he noticed Buck's love for his sons and his completeness with Beth. He yearned to know him better.

Buck reached his arm around Levi's shoulder. "Come look at this." He led Levi along the house to several wooden planks on the ground. He picked up two of the boards. "See what you think of this."

Levi looked into a dark pit. "What do you keep down there?"

"Not too long ago, it kept all of us!" Levi's eyes widened. "This was our dugout. Until I could get enough cattle sold to buy lumber, this is where we lived. Sure makes the headquarters look good, doesn't it?"

"The headquarters?" Levi asked.

Buck pounded on the dwelling. "It's what we call our two-room castle. It's centrally located on the land, so I thought the name fit. Taking a gander into that hole again sure brings back some hard memories. I don't miss sod walls."

"Yes, sir, I'm sure it does bring back hard memories." Levi tried to imagine a family of four living in the ground.

"And that's not the half of it. This is actually the second house we built. Do you see that charring near the foundation?" Levi noticed the darkened wood. "We were out sowing some winter wheat and forgot the cat was left inside the house. That pesky feline knocked our lantern over and burned the whole place to the ground!" Buck leaned against the wall. "I've never wanted to kill a cat so badly in my life. We scavenged what we could from the fire. It was the worst feeling in the world to know we had to go back into this dugout for another year until we made enough on the cows to rebuild."

"It looks like you are doing well now."

"This is why we are here." Buck motioned toward the horizon. "We left it all behind to come here."

"Why?"

Buck looked into Levi's curious eyes. "We wanted to raise our own crops and cattle. We wanted to raise our families on our own land." Buck reached down and gathered a handful of soil. With a prideful stance, he extended his open palm. "We got a chance in Oklahoma."

Levi opened the cabin door carefully balancing a plate of food. He saw Peter lying in bed with his head turned away and placed the plate near his pillow.

"He was asleep when we came in," a voice from the bunk stated. Levi noticed a tall, thin man approach him. "Howdy, I'm Owen Tisdale. You two must be the brothers that Deacon told us about."

Levi shook Owen's hand. "Mr. Samson was kind enough to let us stay here. Are we in the right bunks?"

"Sure. If you had taken Cole's bunk, he would have moved your belongings." Owen pointed at the farthest bunk. Levi looked at an older man, much larger than Owen, resting on his bunk reading a book. The man turned slightly to acknowledge Levi. "That's Cole Berenger. He's the right-hand man around here. You don't want to cross him."

"Does your brother eat in his sleep?"

"I'm sorry, what did you say?" Levi asked, realizing Cole was speaking to him.

"Your brother." Cole pointed at Peter. "Is he going to eat that food or not?"

"If he's asleep, I guess not," Levi replied.

"Owen, fetch me that pan of vittles. And keep your fingers where I can see them."

"Good grief, Cole. I think you'd eat the dwelling if it weren't nailed down." Owen took the plate to him. "I ain't your housekeeper. And don't think I am fetching you anything to drink, either." Levi readied for bed and pulled the sheet to his chest. "You ever drive any cattle?" Owen asked Levi.

"No, we farm, mostly."

"Farmers, huh?"

"My family is. Can't say it appeals much to me. But, I do what I must to help out." Levi watched Owen return to his bunk. "Say, uh, who did you call 'Deacon' a while ago?"

"The Deacon! That's what we call Buck, or Mr. Samson, to you. He got that nickname a long time ago, didn't he Cole? In fact, I bet ole Cole would be happy to explain it to you."

Cole closed his book. "That's enough jabbering. Get to sleep."

Levi rested peacefully on the bunk, thrilled to have the soft support instead of the hard ground. He reached for his journal. He ran his finger across his grandmother's writing. He turned to the next page before realizing the previous page had been ripped away. Puzzled, he closed the journal. He took a last look at Peter and collapsed onto the pillow. The men extinguished their lanterns, allowing the moon and stars to fill the cabin with a pale glow. Levi drifted into a desperate sleep as Peter quietly stared at the cabin wall.

Levi stepped from the door and strolled toward the headquarters. Birds chirped their welcome to the morning and the rising sun. The sky stretched in colored swaths of amber and violet that highlighted the clouds. The peace of the morning brought a newness that he felt in his soul. Not having to prepare for a cross-country journey allowed him to appreciate the beauty of the prairie morning. The soft wind caressed his face. He gave a silent prayer of thanks for the sight before him and entered the house.

The aroma of fresh biscuits and sugar-cured ham was throughout the dwelling. Fried potatoes filled a bowl in the center of the table. Rachel and Matthew focused upon the meal as though it was Christmas morning. A small jug of warmed sorghum syrup complimented the biscuits. Matthew snatched a drizzle of the syrup on his finger and plunged it into his mouth. His eyes glazed in sweet bliss. Beth set a pitcher of fresh buttermilk on the table, causing everyone to gather.

"I'm sure you all can appreciate a hot bowl of grits with those biscuits, can't you?" Beth asked and presented the meal. The children stared at the bounty before them. Ann expressed her gratitude to the Samson family.

"Where is Peter?" Ann asked Levi.

"I thought he was here. He wasn't in his bunk."

Ann looked around the room. "We're not going to wait and let this wonderful meal get cold. Save a seat for him."

Buck placed a heavy chair at the head of the table near Levi. "Have a seat. You and your family are our guests. Matthew, I'll bet you can say a prayer that makes the angels envious."

Matthew blushed. He looked around the room at the new faces waiting for his response. Ann nodded her encouragement. He bowed his head. "Thank you, Lord, for this day. Thank you for these nice people and their nice house. Thank you for this very nice food. And Lord, please let me have a biscuit with sorghum all to myself. Amen."

Ann glared at Matthew. Everyone in the room raised their heads in laughter. Buck chuckled with a hearty tone. "My goodness, Beth. Make sure that young'un gets a biscuit and syrup. We sure don't want the Lord to have to get involved!" Everyone kept laughing and began their breakfast.

"Why don't your ranch hands eat with us?" Rachel asked.

"They keep to themselves and make their own meals. They stay in the cabin," Buck replied. "How was your night out there, Levi? Did you get some good sleep?"

Levi swallowed a large piece of ham. "Yes, sir. Best sleep I've had in weeks. Much obliged."

"Good. I was…" Buck was interrupted by a knock on the door.

Daniel opened the door to see Owen with a solemn expression. "I found this on the floor by his bunk." Owen handed Daniel a folded piece of paper and left.

Daniel read the name and handed it to Ann. Ann opened the paper and read the scribbled writing. She lowered her head and gasped. Beth reached for her hand as Ann looked out of the window. "Peter is gone."

4

The two families gathered by the barn. Buck counted the horses eating in the corral. "Yep. We're short one," he stated.

Owen rested his arms across the wooden fencing. "I heard the horses moving about last night. I didn't know it was your boy."

Levi stepped near Ann. "Our saddle is missing too. It was our only one."

"I know that!" Ann snapped. "It's a saddle. We can get another saddle. It may take ten years to save the money, but we can get another saddle. What I can't get is my son!"

Buck approached Ann. "Tell me again, Ms. Rowe. What did the letter say?"

Ann held the torn paper tightly in her hand. "He says he doesn't want to be here. There is nothing for him here." Ann exhaled a partial laugh. "Then he writes for me to not worry. Imagine that! My son telling me not to worry as I have no idea where he is, what he is doing, or if he is even alive!" Ann threw the wadded letter at Buck's feet. "I'm losing my family." Beth caressed Ann's shoulders and guided her to the house.

"I'm sorry I didn't know any better. I thought the kid had to pee," Owen exclaimed.

"That young man knew what he was doing." Buck walked to Levi standing by the fence watching the horses. "Are you okay? I'm sure your mother didn't mean to take it out on you."

"Peter didn't want to come here. I don't think any of them wanted to."

Buck leaned against the fence. "What about you?"

"I couldn't wait to get here. I wanted nothing to do with that place anymore." His lip quivered.

"Was that your home?"

"Not anymore!" Levi shouted.

"So you wanted more?"

"Yes. I want a life! I want what was taken from me!"

Buck stretched his arm around Levi. "And so does your brother Peter."

Levi was speechless. Buck's words resonated within him as he suddenly felt a connection with his brother. "We both wanted to leave. We just wanted to leave for different reasons."

"Mothers don't take kindly to their sons leaving. But your brother is doing what he must. Pray for him. Pray for his safety. And pray for your family." Buck smacked Levi on the back with an encouraging smile. "I'm going to check on your mother."

Levi watched Buck walk toward the headquarters. He had never heard a man mention praying before, except for their preacher at church. Buck appeared strong and confident, like many men he had known in his life. But his kindness and spiritual fervor exhibited uniqueness. Buck left an impression upon Levi. He observed through Buck that no matter the audience or circumstance, there was strength in faith and in simply being nice.

Levi ventured around the ranch and thought about Peter. The farming equipment, horses, fences and structures alluded to the money and work Buck and his ranch hands invested. Various crops stretched into the distance. Levi walked along the edge of Deep Red Creek. The tranquil beauty of the land calmed him. He heard the giggle of children ahead. He looked through the trees and saw Rachel and Matthew throwing rocks in the water. The two children played without regard for the world around them. Levi admired their innocence, wondering if they were aware of Peter's absence. He hid behind a tree and reached for a rock. He threw the stone toward the children, soaking their feet as it splashed next to them.

"We see you, Levi!" They split up and ran through the trees. Levi took off after them. They ran along the creek bank, stopping to wet their hands. He paused behind a large cottonwood and jumped to the other side.

"I've got you!" he yelled and saw Matthew kneeling. "What are you doing?" Matthew turned and flung a red, round ball of mud at Levi. The sticky pie smeared across his head. "Why you little…"

Matthew exerted a hearty belly laugh and took off through the bushes. Levi pursued. He wiped his eyes to see Rachel emerge from the bank and launch a volley toward him. The earthen cake splattered across his chest and arms. Levi stopped at the sound of joyous chuckles. The children reloaded with dripping mud balls. "Come and get it!" Rachel teased.

The siblings wrestled and played for hours. The heat of the day posed little factor as they refreshed in the cool stream. The steady breeze tried in vain to dry their clothes. They ventured deeper into the woods and followed the creek walking barefooted in the shallow current. The concern for the day amounted to little while they flooded their minds with recreation. The distinct sound of a whistle interrupted their leisure.

"I'll go see who it is," Levi volunteered. "Maw is not going to be happy when she sees our clothes." Levi walked through the tree line and waved at Buck approaching on horseback.

"There you are. I was wondering where you got off to. I sure hope your sister and brother aren't far behind." Buck whistled again. Rachel and Matthew ran through the woods. "Look at you two. You look like you got wet and started to rust. Your mother will have to soak you for a week to get that red earth off you." Buck smiled at the delight on their faces. It had been many years since he had enjoyed the elation of children. "You know what? Since you all aren't afraid to get dirty, I've got something to show you." Buck galloped farther up the bank with Levi and the children following. They approached a bend in the creek joined by a fence across the field. Buck dismounted and motioned for the children to join him.

"What is it, Mr. Samson?" Matthew asked.

"Watch this." Buck cupped his hands together and took a deep breath. He leaned back and bellowed a nasally roar. *"Maa! Maa!"*

"You sounded like a cow," Rachel joked.

"I know. Look yonder." He pointed through the trees.

"Wow!" Matthew exclaimed as thirty black cows hurried toward them. "It's a stampede!" The children watched the cows trot closer and stop a few feet from the fence. Some of the cows slowed their approach. Buck called to them again. The children attempted unsuccessfully to imitate him with calls resembling wailing calves. The herd stared at the children with a puzzled expression.

"Why are they looking at us like that?" Rachel asked.

"They think we're going to feed them. They want to eat," Buck replied.

"Can we pet them?" Matthew asked eagerly.

"Of course." Buck helped Matthew reach over the fence.

"They sure are big."

"And stinky too!" Rachel added.

"Can we ride one?" Matthew inquired.

"Aren't you two the mischievous ones! I bet your mother is plumb exhausted at the end of each day. No, you can't ride one. They would not take kindly to you bouncing around on their backs. They'd throw you like a sack of beans."

"I bet I could ride one. I bet I could ride him all the way to those mountains we saw," Matthew challenged.

"You two remind me of some other youngsters I've heard of. Only they took a ride much farther than the Wichita Mountains."

"Who are they?" Rachel asked and tossed some grass to the cows.

"I heard about it the last time I was in Frederick, Oklahoma. It's a town west of our ranch. Have you ever heard of the Abernathy boys?" Buck asked. The children shook their heads. "They are about your ages and just as mischievous as the two of you." Buck rubbed Matthew's hair. "One day, their father had to go to New York City. It's way up north, far, far away from here. And the boys wanted to go too. So, they decided to hop on horseback and the two of them rode their horses from their home near Frederick all the way to New York City! They did it all by themselves."

"Did their maw spank them when they got there?" Matthew asked.

"No, I don't reckon she did. They were very brave. But, don't you two go getting any ideas. Your poor mother has had enough. Rachel, do you think you and your brother could walk Big G back to the barn for me? I want to talk to Levi while we walk home."

"Do you mean it?" Rachel cheered.

"Sure. Go on. Go slowly. I'll be watching you. Before long, you'll be riding horses." Rachel radiated as she took the rein and walked Big G with Matthew begging for a turn.

"You've got some good siblings there," Buck stated.

Levi watched them argue over the horse. "They are a handful, but I love 'em."

"I can see that." Buck motioned for Levi to walk with him. "Beth and I had a long talk with your mother. She is a strong woman. She would have to be to come up here like you all did." He looked at Levi. "Now, I don't mean to say she didn't come up here without a man. I know you are. And, I must say, I am surprised at her wanting to stay here, especially under the circumstances. Anyone else would have high-tailed it back to where they came from." Levi continued walking along, pondering Buck's narrative. "But, she said several times she wants to stay on your grandparents' land."

"I don't know how we are going to do that. We don't even have money for food. If it weren't for you and Mrs. Samson, I don't know what we would have done." Levi kicked the dirt.

"Yes, that is true." Buck paused. "Which is why I would like for you to work for me."

"Really?"

"Yes. I pay a good wage for a good day's work. And we work around here, you can be sure of that. Your mother agreed to let me pay her to graze my cattle on her land and help to build you all a house. We will need to clear the land, but the more hands the better."

"You would do that for us?" Levi asked.

Buck placed his hand on Levi's shoulder. "It's more than that, son. Folks take care of each other around here. Sometimes it's the only means of making it through the day. You get a job, earn a wage, your family can build for their future and I can expand my herd. We all help each other. And, with the help of the good Lord, we just might make it through the day!"

Levi extended his hand. "Thank you, Mr. Samson, for everything. And thank you for the job."

They approached the barn as the children tied the horse and ran toward the headquarters. "Speaking of future, I guess you plan on taking care of your family?" Buck asked.

"Like you said, Mr. Samson, I'm making it through the day."

Buck observed Levi's solemn avoidance of his question. "Sometimes that is all we have until the Lord opens a door for us." Buck mounted his horse. "I tell ya what. Run into the barn and grab the first horse you see with a saddle and meet me over there by the Deep Red."

Levi entered the barn. A tall, stout horse was tied and saddled. He untied the rein and led the horse outside. The sun magnified its bay coat, highlighting the rich blends of reds and browns. The horse stepped to the side and lowered its head. They appeared to notice each other, meeting eye to eye. The horse reared slightly as Levi extended his open hand. The large animal tossed its head in retaliation, unknowingly shoving its ear into Levi's hand. Levi reacted and scratched behind the horse's ear. It calmed immediately, relaxing its stance while taking a step toward Levi.

"Looks like we found a weak spot," he teased. He slung his leg over the saddle and steadied his mount. He leaned forward and scratched behind both ears. The horse raised its head in jubilant acknowledgment. Levi patted it on the neck and urged the animal forward.

"Looks like the introductions went well," Buck yelled. Levi rode alongside Buck. "That's a fine mount. I bought him from the army when he was younger. He's a good horse, but a bit temperamental. I learned that to calm him down you have to—"

"Scratch behind his ears?" Levi interrupted.

Buck chuckled. "Looks like you two are getting acquainted."

"What's his name?"

"I named him Arrow. He's as fast and straight as an arrow when he runs."

"Arrow," Levi repeated and rubbed its firm neck.

"Come on. You can get to know your mount while I show you around."

"I wish he was my mount. I could only dream to have a horse like this," Levi replied.

"I guess your dream just came true. As long as you work for me, he's yours. You're going to need a good horse around here. So get to know him and take care of him."

Levi placed his hand on the beautiful animal. "Hello, Arrow." He patted it again with newfound admiration.

They rode across the creek through the trees on the other side. The land appeared freshly cleared from undergrowth. Across a small rise, four men steered plow horses in a staggering formation. They carved the earth in unison, turning rows of dirt in preparation for planting. The open area appeared vast, stopped only by the tree line bordering the creek. Levi witnessed the hard work it took to rid the land of mesquite trees and vegetation. He followed Buck to the small rise and dismounted with him.

"Look out from here." Buck pointed toward the tree line. "You can see this is a good vantage point." Levi noticed the spectacular view of the valley and the creek as it twisted along. "We turned this part of the land last spring and found some Indian artifacts. Logan found some tools made out of bone. Owen, my ranch hand, found a rock bowl and what looked like a granite rolling pin. I asked one of the settlers south of us if they had found anything like this on their land. They said there is this Wichita medicine man that lives around these parts. He's a wanderer. They say he shows up here and there. He said this location dates back to the Wichita tribe, one of the first tribes in this area before the reservations." Buck removed his cowboy hat and wiped the sweat from his brow. "I don't know how they know that. That Indian feller can't speak any English, from what I hear."

"This is really interesting," Levi stated. "How long did it take you to clear this land?"

"We started clearing it the day we settled here. I took on Cole and Owen shortly after that, and we have been farming it ever since. We had some settlers passing through a few years back that helped us for a spell. We traded work for some hot meals. We got a lot done in those few weeks."

"It seems like you help a lot of folks around here." Levi guided Arrow off the rise and climbed on to the saddle.

"We've learned to accept whatever the good Lord sends our way, whether it's people or property." They rode across the field toward the Deep Red Creek. Buck let Big G get a drink from the cool stream. "Look at this."

Levi led Arrow to the water. "Are those seashells?"

"They're mussel shells. They are scattered all over the banks of this creek. I'm guessing the Indians came down to the creek and ate the mussels. We've found some other Indian items along the creek banks too."

"I guess you aren't the first folks to live here after all," Levi commented. "There is a lot of history here."

"They were here before us. No matter who got here first or last, we are all just borrowing the land until our time is done."

"I wonder if they thought that too," Levi said.

They led their horses across the creek as Buck continued showing Levi the property. They rode for an hour talking about family, the land, and the work that demanded their attention. The expanse of one hundred sixty acres proved to be overwhelming for Levi. The ride finished where it began. The two men dismounted near the barn and unsaddled their horses. "We start work at sunrise. You can call the cabin your home until we can make other arrangements. What talents did you provide at your homestead?"

"I'd hardly call it talent," Levi jested. "I farmed, mostly."

"Good. Farming is life. Without it, not much happens except a lot of starving. You saw the field my boys and my ranch hands are working. You can start there tomorrow. Then we'll talk about getting your family's house started." Buck continued, "Have you worked with cattle before?"

"No, sir. I wouldn't know the first thing about cows."

"You will." They neared the house and kicked the dirt off their boots.

"Thanks again, Mr. Samson. We are very grateful. And thanks for the horse too."

"We're glad to know you all. And don't forget, we have worship here every Sunday. Work is important, but faith is vital."

The wind became steady as the afternoon sky congested with thick clouds. The northwest view displayed a gray skyline that became more pronounced with each gust. Leaves tossed and the trees whistled while the cool wind surged across the land. The reprieve from the heat rejuvenated the children as they continued their exploration along Deep Red Creek.

"Matthew, I found them!"

Matthew saw his sister near two dirt mounds. "Are you sure?"

"Of course I'm sure. Look." She pointed at the etched markings on the headstones.

"This is a long way from Mr. Samson's house. I wish we had a house."

"We will. Mr. Samson said he is going to help Maw and Levi build one. Maw wants to build it near the graves. She doesn't want them to be forgotten."

"I hope we build it close to the creek. We can play near our house." Matthew picked at the dirt with a stick.

"It will be easier to fetch water too." Rachel looked toward the sky. "We better get home. It looks like a storm's coming."

"I wanted to see the cows again."

"We can next time. Come on," Rachel urged.

Ssscuff! Ssscuff!

"Did you hear that?" Matthew asked.

"Come on, Matthew."

"It's got to be one of Mr. Samson's cows! It must have wandered off." Matthew walked toward the brush and threw his stick into the foliage.

A dark mass moved behind some shrubs. "There it is!" Matthew yelled in excitement. "Watch this." He cupped his hands and bellowed. *"Maa! Maa!"* He stared for a moment and then looked at Rachel. "Maybe it's stuck in the—"

Grruff! Matthew screamed as the large object smashed through the brush. He ran toward Rachel as she hurried away for the open field. Matthew abruptly stopped. He watched in amazement as a massive animal observed him.

"Oh, wow!" Matthew hollered. "Rachel, do you see that? That's the biggest cow I have ever seen!"

"Matthew, run! That cow is not behind a fence. It could charge you!"

The children hustled into the trees and followed the winding creek to the Samson ranch. "Come on. We have to tell Mr. Samson one of his cows is out. Maybe we will get to ride the horse this time!" Matthew said.

The children made their way to the headquarters. Out of breath, they flung the door open and were met by Beth tending the kitchen. "Whoa! What has got you both in such a stir?"

Rachel pushed past Matthew as he wrestled to be first. "Mrs. Samson, we saw a cow over by our grandparents' graves! I think it got out."

"Really?"

"I saw it first, Mrs. Samson! Rachel ran off like a scared cat. It was as big as…as a cow!" Beth giggled. "That certainly sounds big. Let's go tell Mr. Samson."

"I know where it's at. So, Mr. Samson will need to take me on his horse to go find it," Matthew voiced proudly.

"We'll see what Mr. Samson says." They rushed out of the house toward the barn. All of the men were working feverishly to secure the animals as the winds and lightning intensified.

"Beth! You and the children get inside. That storm will be here any minute," Buck hollered from the corral.

"Buck, the children say they saw a cow on the loose!"

Buck placed his hand to his ear, unable to hear. Concerned for the approaching front, he yelled a closing remark. "We've got to get these horses in!"

Beth surrendered the hopeless conversation. "Children, let's get back in the house. This lightning is getting bad and the men need to finish their work. Hurry now." Another strike lit up the sky. The children surrendered and reluctantly followed Beth in to the headquarters.

Rain pounded on the wood-shingled roof. Night arrived early from the thunderstorm blocking the evening light. Lightning continued to streak across the sky with thunder rumbling various items throughout the house. The warm beef stew and fresh bread from supper settled in their bellies. The two families nestled peacefully near the hearth. The fire simmered with cooking coals that invited a gradual slumber across the audience.

"It's really coming down out there," Logan exclaimed.

"The whole place will be a mud bog by morning. I guess plowing the rest of the back acres will be on hold a few days," Daniel presumed.

Buck rested in his rocking chair. "We needed the rain. This will give us time to go get that seed and not lose a day of plowing." Logan and Daniel smirked at each other. They waited patiently for what their father's statement would eventually lead to. "I guess we'll need to go to—"

"Frederick! We're going to Frederick tomorrow?" Daniel shouted.

"Yes. We will leave in the morning." The boys applauded while Buck addressed Beth and Ann. "Ladies, if you will think of the items we need, we can make a day of it."

"That sounds nice," Beth agreed. "We haven't been to town in several weeks. We do need some things."

"It's settled, then. We'll go at sunup."

"Yahoo!" Daniel cheered.

Buck pointed at Daniel. "All right, you. Calm down or I'll stuff you back in that lion's den."

"What?" Levi asked.

Beth entertained Levi. "That's what Buck teases Daniel about. He is named after Daniel in the Bible."

"Oh," Levi replied. "Is that your favorite person in the Bible?"

"I guess you could say that. We named him Daniel for his faith and strength. When life becomes a lion's den, have the faith and strength of Daniel. Then, Lord willing, you can walk out unscathed," Buck explained.

"What about Logan's name?" Levi inquired.

Beth reached for Buck's hand and held it. "Logan is the name of a man that was a good friend to me. In many ways, he saved me," Buck said.

"What did he save you from?"

Buck focused upon the fire. "Myself."

"And he pulled you from the lion's den?"

Buck faced Levi and smiled. "No. God did that."

"You've done well, Mr. Samson." Ann said.

"It wasn't all my doing. Without the help of my family, my two ranch hands and the guide of the Lord, this would all still be untamed grassland. We settled here the first year they opened the Big Pasture, and we drove forty head of cattle from Hennessey, Oklahoma, to start the herd. It was a tough beginning, but we have managed. At one point, I thought disease was going to wipe out the entire herd." Buck settled into nostalgia. "Do you all remember that time Big G injured his leg? It was our second year here and we asked around for anyone that could doctor animals. Someone must have sent that Wichita medicine man to us. He couldn't speak any English, but he sure knew what he was doing. He boiled some bark and berries and mixed this remedy. I watched him put it on Big G's leg and it healed him within a week. Strangest thing I have ever seen. But, it worked."

"Maybe you should hire him on?" Levi joked.

"Yeah. That would be good. But, no one knows where he lives. Someone might see him walking along in a pasture or resting under a tree. That's the only way to find him, from what I hear. But no one has seen him in a while." Buck stoked the fire. He sat in his rocker and faced Rachel and Matthew. "Beth tells me you two found something of your own today?"

"Yes sir, we sure did!" Rachel exclaimed, desperately waiting her turn to speak.

"Hush up, Rachel! I saw it first!" Matthew shoved Rachel aside and crawled next to Buck. "Mr. Samson, we were at the graves where my grandparents are buried and I saw this big cow jump out of the bushes. It scared my sister and she ran off."

"You did too!"

Matthew ignored Rachel. "I did just like you showed us and did my cow call. Once it heard my call it came running."

Buck grinned at the enthusiasm flowing from the children. "That sounds like an adventure."

"I thought you might want to go round it up, but that storm blew in and it got late." Matthew exhibited his discouragement. "But if you want me to show you where it is, we can ride out there in the morning on your horse!"

"You just want to ride his horse," Rachel countered.

"Hush up, Rachel!"

Buck laughed at their competition. "My ranch hand, Owen, got a final count before he turned in today. He said all of our cows are right where they should be. Are you sure you didn't see a coyote? There are lots of them around here."

Matthew frowned. "No. I don't know how to do a coyote call."

Everyone in the room laughed. Rachel and Matthew got upset as Buck consoled them. "I'm sure that whatever you saw was just passing through. Sometimes folks may lose a horse or a stray cow that wanders off from their herd. We'll get there sometime and see if it is still around. If it is, we'll rope it and bring it to the ranch."

"You better have a big rope," Matthew responded. "His horns and neck would probably pull you off your horse!"

Buck's eyes widened, and Logan and Daniel looked at Matthew. "It had horns?"

"Yes, sir. And a big back that went up high like this and down to its bare hind legs."

"Were the horns long and crooked?" Buck asked.

"No, they were short and curved. Kind of like the powder horn that my uncle has for his gun." Matthew imitated the horns with his fingers bent along each side of his head.

"And it had a big back on it?" Logan chimed in.

"Yes. Like it had ten pillows shoved under a brown quilt."

Logan looked at Buck in disbelief. Buck leaned toward Matthew and Rachel. "You two may have seen a buffalo."

"What's a buffalo?" Rachel asked.

"They are actually called *bison*, but folks around here call them *buffalo*. From what you are describing, it sounds like you saw one."

"Is that possible, Pop? Out here?" Logan asked.

"Not too long ago this was buffalo country. Millions of them roamed this area and the Great Plains. Folks say they were hunted to near extinction."

Ann rose from the gathering. "I know two young ones that had better let someone know where they are going next time. Now come on, it is time for bed."

"But, what about the buffalo? Can we go see it tomorrow?" Matthew pleaded.

"Mr. Samson can handle the buffalo. Let's go, both of you. I'm going to turn in as well. Good night and thank you for the wonderful meal." Ann led her anxious children from the room. "Good night, son."

"Good night, Maw," Levi responded. He kissed Rachel and Matthew, and then listened to the developing debate with the Samsons.

"Come to think of it, I remember seeing a small herd of something when we drove those cattle down from Hennessey years back. We never got a good look at them, but some of the hands thought they saw buffalo grazing north of our trail," Buck continued.

"How could buffalo survive with all these settlements and towns now?" Logan asked.

"All they need is grass and water. Given the right area, they could survive just about anywhere," Buck replied.

"Do you want to go see if it is still there in the morning, Pop?"

"No. If it was a buffalo it is probably long gone by now. And it needs to be. Those animals are strong and wild. They could destroy our fences. Let's get to bed. We've got an early journey to Frederick in the morning."

Everyone bid their wishes for a good night. Levi walked to the cabin and sat on his bunk. He looked at the empty bunk across from his bunk and thought of Peter. He wondered where he could have gone. Cole and Owen were already asleep. He adjusted the lantern and reached for his journal. Recalling the events of the day, he collected his thoughts. He looked out of the window and saw the stars glistening in the night. The crisp air was clean from the intense washing by the thunderstorm. The vividness of the universe provoked his imagination. He changed from a format of simply listing the day's events in his journal. Compelled by a newfound desire, he breathed life into a story that captured the essence of the moments. Minutes turned to hours that welcomed a yearning passion to write.

5

The late autumn sun highlighted the golden grasses that extended to the horizon. The contour of the land leveled between occasional slopes in the terrain. The view portrayed a limitless landscape of native vegetation swaying in the breeze. The vastness echoed a sense of solitude that could only be rivaled by oceans. Every direction seemed identical with few landmarks to guide the way. An island of buildings nestled in the distance. The man-made structures beckoned for recognition upon the endless plains.

The two wagons rolled eagerly into Frederick, Oklahoma. The families rejoiced at the overdue sight of civilization. The remote settlement bustled at its own pace with commerce and agricultural commodities. Since its merger from the former towns of Hazel and Gosnell, Frederick became an epicenter for farmers and ranchers settling the Big Pasture and southwest Oklahoma. The families watched the wagons, businesses, and people that went about the Great Plains town.

"I want to see the railroad, Levi! Mr. Samson said the train comes to Frederick," Matthew insisted.

"I know, Matthew. You've been saying that ever since we left headquarters."

"Those tracks have got to be around here somewhere," Matthew continued. "Everyone, listen for the whistle. That means the train is coming. I'm sure it is a big train, big enough to haul all of us across Oklahoma. Make sure the horses don't trip on the tracks, Levi!"

"We have *got* to find that child a train," Ann said.

Levi steered the team to the loading area of the mercantile. The families hopped off the wagons and stretched their legs. Excitement surged through them as they yearned to explore. They entered the mercantile and gazed at the array of goods adorning the shelves. The children were magnetized to the row of colorful sweets imprisoned in the glass candy jars. The women shopped the bounty of fabrics and household items, savoring every moment.

"Beth," Ann inquired. "I need to mail this letter to my brother in Montague County. Would you watch the children for me?" Beth gladly accepted. Ann warned the children of their manners and hurried out of the door.

"Boys, come with me." Buck motioned toward the loading docks. Stacks of bagged seed filled the storage area. Buck counted several bags and pointed their relocation to the wagons. The clerk continued marking off Buck's list while the boys loaded the seed. "Say, do you know of any cattle for sale?" Buck asked the clerk. "I didn't see any on our way into town."

"We're waiting on some from Vernon, Texas. They are selling off several herds down there later this week. There are some good prices, from what I hear. The mercantile proprietor left to go down there today," the clerk said.

"That's good to know. Thank you." Buck admired his growing inventory. He watched another wagon stop near the docks. He glimpsed at an older gentleman stepping from his seat. The two men acknowledged each other in friendly passing. Buck looked at the old man with sudden recognition. He watched him approach the clerk and hand him some money. The clerk motioned for his helpers, and they loaded the old man's wagon with seed. The old man situated his belongings and departed.

Buck pondered the man's face. The past rushed into the present. The recollection swirled within his soul as he remembered the last time he had seen the old man. Consumed with excitement, he approached the clerk again. "Excuse me. Do you know that older feller that just left?"

The clerk looked up from his paperwork. "That was Mr. Wescoat."

"Does he live around these parts?"

"Uh, yeah. I think he has a spread south of here near the Red River. Look, I need to get your order loaded. I've got a train coming in twenty minutes with merchandise. I've got to get to the depot."

Buck paid his bill and steered the wagon around the store to see Levi consoling Matthew. "What's the matter with this young one?"

Levi exhaled. "He's dead set on seeing a train. I keep telling him I don't know when one is coming."

"Is that a fact?" Buck asked with a slight smile. He looked at Matthew's distraught face, recalling fondly the similar expression posed by his own sons when they were Matthew's age. "I tell you what, Matthew. You go and get the women rounded up and into the wagons and we'll see if we can find a train. But you'd better hurry!"

Matthew's solemnness transformed into wide-eyed elation. He ran into the mercantile. "I sure hope you have a plan, Mr. Samson, or that child is going to nag you all the way back home," Levi warned.

The two families paraded around town observing the various establishments. Farmers and ranchers congregated in welcomed interaction before setting out to their acreage. Buck's horses trotted along as lead team. His proposition to find a train instigated new passenger arrangements for each wagon. The children and young men piled into Buck's wagon while Ann and Beth rode casually behind. Matthew's persistence to locate a train led Buck into a developing desperation.

"You know, Mr. Samson," Matthew started another monologue. "If you did your cow call just loud enough, people would think it's a train! Hey, what about those buildings over there? I wonder if the railroad is behind those buildings. I think you should go over—"

"Guess what I heard?" Buck interrupted. "I heard that President Roosevelt actually came to Frederick not too long ago."

"Who?" Matthew asked.

"The president, silly," Rachel scolded.

"Did he ride on the train?" Matthew gleamed.

"Boy, you have certainly got the train on your brain! As a matter of fact, yes. He did come on the train. Folks around here say he came to Frederick to go wolf hunting with the father of those two boys I told you about, the Abernathys. Anyway, the boys' father was known for catching wolves alive. And do you know how he did it?" Buck looked at each child's anticipation. "He caught them in their mouths with his bare hands!"

"Did they bite him?" Rachel asked.

"No. He was that good. Even the president didn't believe it until he saw Mr. Abernathy do it."

"I would have just run over one with a train," Matthew boasted. Everyone laughed as Matthew scowled at them.

"Those Abernathy boys lived around here. Their names were Bud and Temple. This is where they left to go to New York City."

"That's nothing! Anyone can go there on a train," Matthew countered.

"No, remember now, they did it on horseback, all by themselves."

"Were they scared?"

"It was a grand adventure, I'm sure. They are very brave boys." Buck pointed ahead. "Do you see that building up yonder?" Matthew and Rachel turned their attention forward. "That's the train depot."

"That's where the trains are?" Matthew celebrated.

"Matthew! Are you crazy? That's where the train stops. Do you see the tracks on the other side of it?" Rachel directed.

"Ooh! I see 'em. I see the tracks!" Buck stopped near the depot. Matthew jumped from the wagon and ran to the building. The wooden structure stood as a testament to modern transportation. It was massive to Matthew. He stared at the imposing building with its large windows and high, angled roof. The depot appeared longer than it was wide and it complemented the railway. Its construction conveyed prideful craftsmanship with decorative crossbeams at the end of the building. A boarded walkway ran parallel to the tracks. Inside the depot, people began to gather. Buck motioned the children along the walkway. The shimmer of the silver rails glistened into the horizon. The sturdy rail ties cut a pronounced path across the plains. Its visible intrusion appeared as a scar upon the earth.

"Those tracks are big," Rachel stated.

"Can I go see 'em, Mr. Samson?" Matthew asked.

"Sure. That's probably the most admiration these rails have gotten since they were laid." Matthew stood on the first rail. He looked back for anyone watching him. His smile stretched in delight as he walked the metal beam. Rachel hurried to join him on the opposite rail. The two children appeared as though they were walking on tightropes. They moved side by side, giggling to see who would fall off first. Ann watched her children relish the moment. Levi and the boys observed from the shade. Beth exited the depot and hurried toward Buck. She winked at Ann and whispered in Buck's ear.

Buck looked south. "Hey, you two, look behind you."

The children turned around. "What?"

"Follow the tracks and look."

"I see a fire," Matthew observed.

"That's just smoke," Rachel countered.

"Come up here and look again."

The children stood on the wooden walkway and looked into the horizon. "That smoke is getting closer," Matthew noticed.

Buck leaned next to their ears. "Listen…"

The children quieted. The smoke clouded the sky in a streaming, black congestion that thickened with each passing second. They watched with curious attention. Matthew faced Buck. "Is that a…"

Whoop! Whooo!

Buck watched Matthew's eyes widen in jubilation. "Yes, it is."

The vibrant sound pierced the stillness and echoed across the landscape. The oncoming achievement of man-made ingenuity signaled its arrival. A crowd gathered to watch the dark smoke become more concentrated. The children pointed for everyone to see. A circular, silver smokebox became distinguishable against the black pilot that appeared to glide above the rails. The whistle sounded again with rising white steam. A bell tolled as the rhythmic pounding of the engine deepened with a thunderous approach. Steam bellowed all about the engine. The chimney cast the black smoke high above. The headlight glistened while the iron machine clamored closer. The children watched the train slow. Its massive side rods and driving wheels rumbled by. Steam bellowed across the tracks. Buck observed the pleasure in the children's faces. He saw the engineer notice him from the cab. Buck pointed at Rachel and Matthew and signaled the engineer. The engineer greeted Buck with seasoned expectation and focused upon the children. He waved and tugged on the whistle again as the engine and tender rolled passed.

"He waved at us!" Rachel and Matthew hailed. "Maw, did you see? The man driving the train waved at us!"

"Yes, I did. Isn't this wonderful?" Ann approached Buck. "Thank you, Mr. Samson. My children have not had happiness like this for a long time."

"I know."

Ann rejoined with her children.

Beth stood next to her husband. "I love you."

Buck wrapped his arm around Beth and kissed her forehead. He watched the first passenger exit the railcar. "I love…"

Beth looked up at Buck. "What is it?" she asked and turned toward the train.

A tall man with a dark duster and weathered cowboy hat stood at the steps facing Buck. She felt Buck's embrace tighten as he mumbled, "Oh my God."

"Who is that man?" Beth demanded. She watched a sneering grin etch across a corner of the man's chapped lips. He nodded slowly at Buck. Four men approached him from the depot. Each man gave a brief welcome and then joined in the revelation. "Buck, why are those men looking at us?"

Buck kept eye contact with the men. "Get everyone into the wagons. We're going home."

"Buck!" Beth demanded.

"It's nothing, dear. Just looked like someone I have seen before. Let's go." Beth escorted everyone to the wagons. Rachel and Matthew hugged Buck, thanking him for the adventure. He ambled to the corner of the depot and glanced down the walkway. The five men stood in a line staring back at him. Their eyes penetrated his presence. Buck moved briskly around the depot and mounted the wagon. "Boys, I want you to drive the other wagon. And pay attention to what you are doing. Levi, you ride with me." Buck watched the boys adhere to his directions and snapped the reins. "Keep pace with me until I say otherwise, do you hear?" The two wagons hurried east of town, leaving the five men watching from the depot.

The families journeyed back and reminisced about their adventures in Frederick. The children imitated every sound of the steam engine with each passing mile. The highlight of the trip would be shared for many a night's bedtime stories. Each person told their version of the day while Levi listened to his sister and brother from the front seat. Weary of Matthew's repeated version, Levi mustered enough courage to address Buck.

"Mr. Samson, are you all right?"

"What? Yes. I'm fine. Just giving some thought."

"That's funny. Because since we left Frederick, you've looked behind us every half mile. And I assume that mumbling you've been doing is praying?"

"You see a lot. Levi, how would you like to make some real money?"

"Sure."

"We'll get home shortly and I want you to get some sleep. Tomorrow morning, pack your things and saddle your horse. You, the boys, Owen, and I are going to Vernon, Texas."

"Whatever you say, Mr. Samson," Levi replied. "What are we going there for?"

"I'm going to buy some cattle. And then you are going on your first cattle drive."

"Oh," Levi responded, hiding his initial shock.

"Don't worry. I went on my first cattle drive when I was fifteen. It was a heck of a lot farther than Vernon to Big Pasture. We'll have those cattle on the move and home before you know it."

"I'll try not to break a sweat."

"You're gonna sweat. That I can promise you," Buck declared. "Tell your maw and we'll leave before sunup."

"I don't need to tell Maw. I'll be ready."

"I know you are a man, Levi, and you have made your own choices. I meant that you should let your maw know so she doesn't worry."

"I understand."

"You've shouldered the brunt of your family, haven't you?" Buck asked.

"No, sir, my maw has. I don't want to leave them, especially with what happened to my grandparents."

"Leaving them is exactly what you'll have to do. Your maw is a strong woman. She will figure out what she needs to do. As for you, you need to get on with your life."

"I guess so. I just don't know when. I wouldn't know how to start," Levi revealed.

"It's not a matter of knowing, it's a matter of doing. And you will start by going on this cattle drive." He observed the uncertainty in Levi. "I have learned one important thing during my years. It has helped me find both reason and reality. And I can tell you from hard, honest truth that reason and reality are two of the most puzzling things there are." Levi waited in anticipation. "You said it earlier," Buck hinted.

Levi shrugged his shoulders. "I don't recall."

Buck showed an encouraging grin. "Prayer."

The crisp morning air carried a chill that teased of early winter. The leaves began to blanket the ground in swaths of tan and brown. The foliage's attempt to cover the earth proved pointless against the wind. The northern surge whisked away the remnants of fall. Rachel and Matthew ignored the weather and continued following the Deep Red Creek.

"Maw said not to go very far," Rachel reminded.

Matthew ignored his sister. "Autumn sure doesn't last very long in Oklahoma. There were leaves on those trees a while ago." He pointed at the oak grove. "Come on. I want to go see the graves." They journeyed along the bank looking through the undergrowth. Their range of vision extended from the reduced vegetation. Matthew ran up the embankment and stood at the summit.

"You'd better not go far! Remember what Maw said," Rachel warned again. Matthew walked out of sight. Rachel ran after her brother. "Matthew, I'm not chasing after you again!" She reached the top of the embankment to see Matthew sprinting toward her. A huge brown bison charged after him. Matthew screamed as the animal gained on him with each powerful stride. Rachel ran to the nearest tree. She stopped near the oak grove watching Matthew collapse behind her. They peered from behind the oak while the bison lumbered toward them.

"What are we going to do?" Matthew shouted between breaths. The bison lowered its head, appearing to collide with the tree. The children shrieked. The bison suddenly lifted its head and stopped in front of them. It exhaled ferociously in disagreement to their presence. "I think it's scared of the tree."

"Or it's scared of him." Rachel pointed to a man standing near the creek bank. The man held his arm toward the agitated animal and walked toward it.

"That man is going to die!" Matthew shouted.

"Wait," Rachel countered. They watched the man stop a few yards from the bison. The giant creature spied the children a last time and strolled away.

"How did he do that?" Matthew emerged from the tree with Rachel cautiously behind him.

"Thank you, sir. We thought that buffalo was going to get us!" Rachel neared the man.

The man faced them. Matthew spoke in astonishment. "You're an Indian." The man witnessed the children without expression. His chiseled face, weathered and wrinkled from years of exposure, appeared hard and emotionless. His buckskin pants were faded and soiled. The layers of clothing were tattered from extensive use against the elements. He stood tall in stature and surveyed every detail of the children. The trio watched each other in awkward anticipation. The man knelt and extended his arm. He opened his hand revealing a pile of thick, brown fur.

Rachel reached for a sample. "It's hair. I think it's buffalo hair." She looked at the man with a slight smile. Matthew reached to touch it.

"It's rough," he stated. Each child acknowledged the man. He motioned for them to follow and walked to a rise in the field. The children pursued with apprehension.

"Rachel, look!" Matthew pointed at the bison joining a female near the embankment. "What's that behind her?"

Rachel watched a third bison step from behind the female. "It's a baby!"

"They're all there, Mr. Samson. Stay on the trail that I showed you and you'll have plenty of grazing and some water. There aren't any fences along that route, yet. Be careful." The rancher closed the corral gate and wished them farewell.

Buck rode Big G and watched his boys, Levi, and Owen Tisdale gather fifty head of cattle. He observed the moment with serenity. The legacy of driving cattle across the open plain surged within him. Since his boyhood, he grew to love the work of a demanding cattle drive. The sporadic weather, the vast landscape, and a herd of cattle on the move was life in the former territory. The long cattle routes of recent history had already receded in to tales of folklore. The grueling task of moving numerous cows across untamed country was replaced by trains and fences. What was once appreciated as an achievement toward manhood was now reduced to a boy's bedtime story.

He watched his sons work the cows into formation. Owen anchored the group. His veteran experience encouraged the young men to follow his lead. Levi watched Owen, Logan, and Daniel with eagerness. The dust swirled in the December wind. Buck prayed for a safe journey and opened his eyes to see his ranch hands watching him. He boasted a prideful smile feeling the emotion of the moment. He raised his cowboy hat and leaned forward in the saddle. Filling his lungs with air, he bellowed above the constant call of the cattle. "Boys, let's move 'em out!"

"Yee-haw!" Owen yelled and waved his cowboy hat. "All right, you tenderfoots, let's point these stragglers northward!" Owen slapped his hat against his thigh. He looked at Buck, sharing an appreciation of the event. Buck watched the cows begin to migrate. Most of the cattle bunched together with the remainder of the herd in pursuit. Buck nudged Big G into a gallop. He solemnly began what he knew would be his last cattle drive.

The first hours seemed like minutes. Levi led Arrow alongside the herd. What began in dreadful anticipation settled into unbridled adventure. The power of the herd, combined with the agility of Arrow beneath him, brought words that would later fill the pages of his journal. Levi felt united with the land and cattle. What were once fireside stories by veteran cowboys was now a glorious reality for him.

"How are you holding up over there?" Owen hollered across the herd.

"This is great!" Levi answered.

"I've never heard anyone say driving cattle was great."

"Try driving a plow! Believe me, this is great."

Owen bowed in agreement. "For a first-timer, I'd say you are off to a good start. Keep 'em moving toward Logan up front. The Red River is on the other side of that ridge. Once he finds a shallow crossing, we'll steer the herd that way."

The bank of the Red River proved to be a gentle slope. The sparse winter rain provided a passing current a few feet deep at the crossing. The cattle pushed through the water and the thick, red earth without delay. The width of the river basin exceeded the narrow amount of water that flowed through. Levi watched the herd progress from the bank. Seeing the signal from Owen, he guided Arrow into the water. The horse's front hooves sunk into the red soil. The sudden shift in the mud spooked

Arrow. It lunged to escape, launching Levi in to the air. He reached for the reins as Arrow rose onto his hind legs and threw Levi into the river.

The cold water stung his skin, soaking him instantly in the shallow current. Levi gasped for breath and was pulled from the water by his shirt. "Are you okay?" Buck asked and dragged him to dry ground. "That was quite a spill."

Levi coughed. "I can't feel my hands."

"Daniel! Round up some wood and get a fire going. Yell at Owen and bring some blankets." Buck addressed Levi: "Get out of those clothes before you freeze." Buck stripped Levi and covered him in his blanket. Owen arrived and wrapped two more blankets around Levi, rubbing his back to entice circulation. Daniel wadded some brush under a pile of dried driftwood and started a fire. The men carried Levi to the fire and began warming his extremities.

"December is a little chilly for swimming!" Owen jeered.

"His face is blue, Pop," Daniel pointed.

"He'll come around. You get over to Logan. Tell him to pick out ten of our best cows and separate them from the herd. Wait with him until I get there." Daniel encouraged Levi and left for the herd. "Owen, stay with Levi until his clothes dry. The herd should be fine in this valley. We'll go ahead and bed down here for the night. There's plenty of water and I have a bag of beef jerky." Buck watched Levi shiver near the fire. "You'll warm up soon."

"What are you doing with ten cows, Deacon?" Owen asked.

Buck dreaded the question he knew Owen would pose. "I told you I saw him at the mercantile. I know it's him. I am only doing what I should have done years ago."

"Deacon, this is no time to have your conscience get in the way! What's past is past."

"And that past has been haunting me every day since. Watch the boy. We'll be back tomorrow morning." Buck paused. "You did bring what I told you to bring, am I right?"

"Go clear your conscience. We'll survive."

Buck turned Big G toward the Oklahoma side of the Red River. Owen watched him unite with his sons and drive ten cows over the ridge.

Levi began to control his shivering. "I knew I shouldn't have come back to Texas."

The red coals simmered beneath a fresh pile of driftwood. The flames engulfed a steady supply of brush. Levi sat in a warm bundle. He wiggled his toes in relief. His clothes were nearly dry from the heat and nighttime breeze. He held the blankets tightly against his body.

"Here, get some more of this down you." Owen handed Levi another cup of hot coffee. "For a guy that doesn't drink coffee, you sure are making quick work of it."

Levi held the warm metal cup. "Thanks, Owen. I would have been a goner for sure."

"Naw. It's all part of a cattle drive. I've been thrown so many times it's a wonder I can walk." Owen reached for Levi's clothes. "Here. These are dry. Get 'em on. You'll need 'em to get through the night. I never did care for winter cattle drives."

"Can't say that I blame you," Levi grinned. He tore off a piece of jerky and leaned closer to the fire. "Will the cows make it through the night?"

"They're not going anywhere. This river bottom will keep them from wandering too much."

"How many cattle drives have you been on?" Levi asked.

"More than I can remember. I did short drives, mostly. Never had the desire for those cross-country drives that took months to finish and in all kinds of weather."

"It seems like you and Mr. Samson have been doing this a long time."

Owen positioned his sleeping gear. "It depends on which time. The Deacon and I used to not be so honest when it came to cattle."

"How's that?"

"All men have something they would rather forget about their pasts." Not taking the hint, Levi continued to stare at Owen. "You are either stubborn or too innocent." He laughed shortly. "I'll bet on the innocent." Owen gathered his blanket and wrapped it around his overcoat. "Deacon, Cole, and I go way back. We met in a little town called Tombstone in the Arizona Territory."

"Really?"

"We had some wild times, too wild at the end." Owen stared into the night sky. "Have you noticed that limp Cole has?"

"Yeah."

"I can't say I saw it, but the story goes that he was playing poker in Tucson and the game went sour. He got into a scuffle and narrowly missed a bullet to his gut. It ended up grazing his leg."

"Who shot him?" Levi asked.

Owen leaned over. "You ever heard of Doc Holliday?" Levi's mouth dropped open. "Like I said, I never saw it, but that's the story."

"Was he in the gunfight at the OK Corral?"

Owen snickered. "No. That happened later. We were long gone from there by then."

"I heard you and Mr. Samson talking about those ten cows. What is he doing?"

"At one time, we were bad men. We did things we are ashamed of now. Don't ever think you can run from your past. You can't. One way or another, it has a funny way of coming back. Sometimes, it comes back when you don't expect it." Owen progressed with Levi's question. "That is what happened to Deacon. He is taking ten cows to a man we stole from a long time ago."

"Who is the man?"

"What's it matter? When you do something that's wrong and later regret it, it doesn't matter who it is."

Levi debated his next question with temptation encouraging him. "Did any of you ever kill anyone?"

Owen was silent for several seconds. "There was a time I would have been proud to hear that question from someone. If you mean murder anyone, no, none of us ever went that far. We wanted to at times, but that is when Deacon stepped in."

"Why do you keep calling him Deacon?"

"He has a servant's manner. He saved us from ourselves. We once belonged to a bad group of men that rode around the western territories rustling what cattle we could for money. We were about to hit a large ranch one night when some of the men we were with started shooting. A man was killed. We were young and stupid. The next day, Deacon and the leader of the group had words. He tried to split up the group and only Cole and I left with him. There was bad blood between him and the leader."

"Why did you three decide to leave the group?"

"The leader kept pushing everyone to make lots of money fast. He wanted to rustle larger cattle herds. At one time, our group was over twenty men. So one day, the leader goes after this herd near an Indian reservation. Dumbest thing I ever did."

"Why is that?"

"The cattle belonged to the army."

"Whoa. What happened?" Levi urged.

"Our group was reduced to ten within a matter of minutes. I couldn't tell for sure, but it looked like a cavalry regiment was after us. It was as if they were waiting for us. Deacon had enough and started to leave when the leader shot at him. He missed."

"What did Mr. Samson do?"

Owen laughed. "He missed too." Owen relived the history seen only in his mind. "But, Cole didn't. He shot the leader twice in the chest." Levi was paralyzed in silence. "He saved Deacon's life. And then this other guy, kind of like the second in charge, pulled his revolver and aimed at Cole. That's when ole Deacon didn't miss."

"Mr. Samson shot him?"

"That he did. The three of us high-tailed it out of there and never saw those men again. But, it turns out that the man Deacon killed had a brother. It's been many years, but we heard his brother was torn up about the death. I guess most brothers would be."

"Did the brother ever come looking for Mr. Samson?" Levi persisted.

"I don't know." Owen rested his head against the bedroll. "But, he got off the train in Frederick when you all were there the other day."

6

"But, Maw! There was a baby too. Can we go see if it is still there?" Rachel begged.

"Not now. And you stay away from strangers, do you hear? I don't care who this Indian is, you stay away from him," Ann demanded.

"But, Maw…"

"Young lady, you have chores to do and so does your brother. We don't live here, we are invited. We will show our gratitude by helping in every way possible. Do you understand?" Ann continued washing the utensils from breakfast. "Until the men arrive with the cattle, we are going to earn our keep. Now go out to the barn and help your brother."

Rachel moped to the barn. The December wind nipped at her face. The sound of footsteps neared as Matthew ran from the corner of the house.

"You didn't try hard enough," he scolded.

"No help from you! You were hiding outside like a scared cat."

"I'm going to finish my chores and go see it."

"Not if Maw says you can't," Rachel warned.

Matthew opened the corral. "She never said we couldn't go, we just had to finish our chores. So don't go blabbing your mouth about it." They entered the barn and grabbed some shovels. "I hate cleaning the stalls. Horse poop stinks!"

"Mind your manners and do what Maw says. The Samsons are letting us stay here."

"Only until Maw gets enough lumber to start our house. Mr. Samson said that when he gets the cattle here, he'll graze them on our land and then pay Maw. Mr. Samson is smart," Matthew declared.

"Hey." Rachel stopped. "Maybe we could get the baby to graze on our land too. Then we could take care of it!"

"Yeah! That's a great idea. We could move all three of them on to our land just like Mr. Samson's cattle drive. Come on, let's hurry and finish. And don't tell anyone this time!" Matthew threatened.

"Don't tell anyone what?" a voice questioned from behind.

The children spun around to see Cole Berenger tower in the entry. His six-foot-four stature portrayed him as a giant. His presence filled the doorway allowing very little light to penetrate around him. He stepped toward the children with a slight limp.

"You're the biggest man I've ever seen," Matthew announced. "Do you ever hit your head on the doorway?"

"No. But I have stepped on small children before."

Matthew looked at Cole's boots. "Your toes must be huge! Did you crunch them flat when you stepped on them?"

"He's joking, Matthew. I think." Rachel studied Cole.

"Have you two been going on about some bison on the north acreage?" Cole inquired.

"No, sir. We saw three buffalo up that way," Matthew pointed northward. "We saw a maw and a paw and a baby."

"Hush up, Matthew," Rachel interrupted. "Bison *are* buffalo. And you just said not to tell anyone. We don't know him."

"He looks nice to me. What do we call you?"

"You can call me Co…uh, Mr. Berenger."

Matthew whispered at Rachel. "What did he say?"

"His name is Mr. Berenger."

"Wow! I wish I had a name like that. My name is Matthew and this is my sister, Rachel. Sometimes I call her Rae Rae, but not much. No one else calls her that. We live with the Samsons until we can make enough money to build a house. Do you hate shoveling manure?"

"You talk too much," Cole responded. "You had better finish your chores." Cole turned to leave the barn.

"Do you want to go see the buffalo with us?" Matthew asked.

"Maybe some other time."

"Okay. We'll come get you when we finish." Matthew reached for his shovel and hurried to work. Cole watched the children while they completed their chores.

"Mr. Berenger!" Cole leaned out of the entryway to see Beth running toward him. "We've got cows on the loose! I saw several of them grazing by the creek." Beth pointed north of the ranch.

"I'll round them up, Mrs. Samson. We might have a fencing problem again." Cole positioned his horse and grabbed the saddle horn. With a few swift kicks, he guided his mount out of the corral. Rachel and Matthew watched him follow the creek until he was out of sight.

Cole and his horse trotted at a steady pace, looking for cattle. The creek was an ideal gathering place for cows. The December winter had yet to unleash its fury or provide the late annual rains to fill the ponds. The smell of water lured the animals from their pasture grass. Cole reached the first row of fencing and followed it along the creek. He rode to the nearest rise and spied across the treed valley. Six cows grouped along the creek bottom ahead. He prodded his horse toward the cows and herded them up the rise.

Cole enjoyed the cowboy life. Living on a ranch suited his inner calling and accentuated his desire for solitude. The confusion of life convoluted his younger years. What was once a thrill to ride on the edge had matured to watching cattle in peaceful bliss. Working a ranch with the southwestern sun upon his face calmed his life while his soul searched for purpose. The day he followed Buck away from jeopardy led to a life of hope and tranquility. He lived life on his terms, free and in control. But now he wondered.

They strolled on to the flat. Cole guided the cattle toward a large opening in the fence. The cows bounded through the gap and rejoined the herd. Cole dismounted and observed the damaged fencing. He pulled a clump of dark-brown hair from the wiring and studied it. He tucked the hair into his coat pocket and pulled a hammer and some nails from his saddlebag. He repaired the breach while the herd observed the commotion.

He removed the broken post and walked into the woods to locate a replacement. He approached the rise and threw the pieces into the brush.

"Ouch!"

Cole instinctively reached for his hip. Angry at the habit he thought he had forgotten, he yelled into the thicket. "Come out of there!" Holding his hammer, Cole watched a small boy and a little girl crawl from underneath the thorns. "You two!"

"Hello, Mr. Bear. I'm sorry if we scared you. But I didn't think you ever got scared because you are so big. Rachel said we should see if the buffalo are here."

"No, I didn't! You wanted to follow him, you fibber!"

"That's enough!" Cole interrupted. "Did you finish your chores?"

"Yes," the children answered together.

"I find that hard to believe." Uncertain of what to do, he offered all that he could conjure. "Do you two know how to fix a fence?" The children were speechless. "Well, then. You are about to learn. Get into those woods and find me a post big enough to fit that hole in the ground."

"Yes, Mr. Bear. I'll find you one." Matthew ran off picking up every stick he could find.

Cole leaned toward Rachel. "What did he call me?"

"Mr. Bear."

Cole waited for an explanation. Seconds passed with the realization that Rachel had no intention of continuing. "And why is he calling me that?"

"He thinks that's your name. When he can't say things very well, he says what he thinks they sound like."

"He thinks I'm a bear?"

"No." Rachel giggled. "He thinks your name is Mr. Bear Ranger. He really likes your name. Do you mind if he calls you that?"

Cole pondered her question. "I've been called worse."

"Here they come!" Owen shouted from the ridge. Levi directed Arrow up the embankment. "Over that way." He pointed. "You can't miss 'em. They're riding like their tails are on fire." Both men watched as Buck, Logan, and Daniel sprinted across the terrain. "The last time I saw Buck ride like that…"

"What?" Levi asked.

"You stay here." Owen kicked the sides of his horse and rode toward them.

Levi looked at the forty cows positioned along the north bank of the Red River. Logan and Daniel stopped next to him. "How was your detour?" Levi inquired.

"It was good. We delivered the cows to that old man Pop knew and they talked for a while. Looks like you finally got dry. Did you and Owen have any problems?" Logan asked.

"Naw, it was a quiet night. Why were you riding so fast?"

"Pop told us to. When we left that old man's ranch Pop said to ride like the wind. I guess he wanted to get back here fast."

"Hey, you tenderfoots, it's time to work. Let's get these cattle moving," Owen ordered. "Logan, you and Levi take the front. Daniel, we'll stagger between the middle and the rear until Buck comes back."

"Where's Pop going now?" Daniel asked.

"He'll be back shortly. You all get movin'." Owen whistled three times and yelled as loudly as he could. The herd jolted into awareness and bounded up the bank. Owen rode behind the cows and hurried them along.

"I wonder what Pop is doing? He hasn't been right since we left that old man's ranch," Logan told Levi.

"Owen told me why Mr. Samson took those ten cows to that old man. That was really nice of him. Most folks would have just forgotten about it."

Logan looked at Levi. "Forgotten about what?"

"Uh, I thought…Well, what *did* he do with those cows?"

"He said he owed that man ten cows from a long time ago. What did Owen say?" Logan asked.

"Nothing. It must have been about something else."

"Logan, Levi! Keep those cows steady," Owen yelled from behind.

"Logan," Daniel hollered as he rode next to Levi. "What's got Owen so spooked? He's running these cows like a thunderstorm's comin'."

"Boys!" All three young men turned to see Buck pull Big G into a skidding stop near them. "Didn't Owen tell you three to get movin'? It's time to work. Get ready, we're gonna run these cows for a bit. Stay alongside and don't get in the middle of them. I want two of you on each side of the herd. Levi, you come with me on the right, and boys, you take the left. I'm counting on you."

Logan and Daniel acknowledged their father and rode to flank the herd on one side. Levi followed Buck to the opposite side. The cows quickened their pace. Owen whooped and hollered, provoking the herd into a minor stampede. The cows ran with a collective effort. The rumble of their approach cast dust into the air. Unsure of what to do, Levi motioned Arrow into a quick step and followed suit. The power of the herd and the rush of Arrow's speed were exhilarating. He pulled his cowboy hat firmly upon his head and held the reins tightly. He kept farther away from the herd than Buck. The thought of falling off Arrow again intensified his awareness. They drove the herd a considerable distance before Buck waved at Owen. The herd lessened its fervor. Levi slowed Arrow and galloped next to Buck, standing near a tree in stern observation.

"That was quite a ride, Mr. Samson!"

Buck watched the rear of the herd. "Keep them moving. There are some mesquites up ahead. I don't want to lose any of them in the thickets."

"What's the hurry, Mr. Samson?"

"We need to get these cows home as quickly as possible." He looked across the herd again and nudged Big G into a speedy departure.

The herd sustained its trek through the mesquite trees. Levi listened for Owen's continuous whistle. He smashed through some low limbs scratching his face and hands.

"How are you doing over there?" Owen shouted.

Levi grimaced at the thought of Owen watching his engagement with the tree. "I'm herding squirrels at the moment!"

Owen released a hearty laugh. "I think you are starting to understand this cattle driving business." Owen rode to Levi and brushed some leaves off his back. "It's been a great ride so far, hasn't it?"

"I thought cattle drives were slower than this?"

"They are. We needed to get moving, though."

"I can tell," Levi said. "Mr. Samson sure seems on edge."

"He has reason to be. We're being followed."

"By who?" Levi checked behind them.

"Can't say for sure. Deacon saw them when they left old man Wescoat's house. You stay on this side of the herd and keep them tight. And no stragglers."

They urged the herd forward as night hastened. The chilly December air bit at them with their layered clothing. The setting sun revealed a clear sky that threatened a cold night. Levi squinted to see across the backs of the cattle and search for the men on horseback. The onslaught of cold and hunger decreased his stamina. The path ahead darkened with uncertainty.

The cows' mooing began to dissipate. Levi attempted to distinguish the approaching sound of horse hooves.

"Levi, how are you doing?" Buck asked.

"I'm fine, sir. I'm sure missing your fireplace, though."

"We all are. Here's the plan. There is a small wash up ahead. We're going to hold up there for the night. I've got Logan riding ahead to start a fire. It will be down in the wash so you won't be able to see it at first."

"Who's following us, Mr. Samson?"

Buck hesitated. "You don't worry about that. When we get the herd to the wash we'll take shifts two at a time. There won't be much sleep tonight, but we can stay as warm as we can. Daniel is going to keep the fire going and warm us some food. Owen and Logan will take first watch, and then you and me. Get some sleep as soon as you get settled."

"Yes, sir." Levi noticed the outline of a revolver holstered against Buck's leg. "Are you expecting any trouble?"

Buck pulled his duster over his thigh. "Son, when it comes to moving cattle across open territory, I expect anything."

"Levi, wake up."

Levi felt a boot nudge him from a deep sleep. The nighttime air weighed heavily over his face. "I'm awake."

Owen pulled the blanket from Levi's spot. "It's your watch. Buck is waiting for you. Here, drink this hot coffee before you mount. It'll help peel the sleep off your eyes. And take this. I'm guessing you know how to use it?"

Levi strained to see a revolver strapped securely inside a leather holster. "What do I need that for?"

"Hopefully nothing."

Levi downed the hot coffee and greeted Daniel, who handed Levi a fresh cornbread biscuit with warm, salt-cured ham. He wolfed the fireside meal in three huge bites and drank another cup of coffee. Daniel tossed him an extra biscuit. Levi waved his appreciation. The two boys wished each other well as Levi hurried toward Buck. "Aw! I forgot my saddle."

"You need to rub that sleep from your eyes. Look at your horse."

Levi checked Arrow, surprised to see him saddled. "Thank you, Mr. Samson. You didn't have to do that."

"I didn't. A rule of courtesy on my cattle drives is that the team going off watch saddles the next team's horses. It makes for a better beginning to your watch. Now get mounted. The good thing about our watch is we'll get to see the sun come up."

Levi followed Buck to the cattle. The cows nestled in a tight group along the base of the wash. The sides of the ravine rose above their heads, obscuring their presence from level ground. Unsure of how to keep his first watch, he rode next to Buck and waited for instructions. Their distance from the fire exposed a consuming blackness. Levi watched for any outlines of trees or shrubs. A streak of light caught his attention. He looked up to see millions of shining specks glisten across the sky. The numerous stars cleared his vision. He stared at the heavenly spectacle. Another shooting star streaked from the north, leaving a beam of light across the horizon.

Moo! Levi jumped from the cow next to him. Its thick hide rubbed against his leg, causing Arrow to stir. He pulled the reins and guided Arrow into another cow on the opposite side. Arrow began to fidget. Levi panicked. Suddenly, Arrow rose on his back legs at the sight of a large bull. "Whoa! Easy, boy!" Arrow bucked again, forcing Levi nearly off his saddle. "Whoa, Arrow, whoa!"

Levi felt his seat give way and he slid from the saddle. A forceful tug along his collar stopped his fall. He repositioned his boot in the stirrup and regained his balance. The tug thrust him back into his saddle. He twisted to see Big G nudge Arrow. The two horses calmed and turned away from the irate cattle. Levi felt the tug release followed by a brisk slap across his back. "I bet you'll pay attention from now on, eh, cowboy?"

"Sorry about that."

"No harm done, this time. But let that be a lesson. Out here, some mistakes can cause a stampede, get you thrown from your mount, or worse—get you killed, or get another cowhand killed. And, no matter what, no sleeping on watch. If there is a cardinal sin to night watch, that's it."

"Yes, sir. I guarantee I am awake now."

Levi followed Buck to the slope and watched the herd in the pale light. The first hour passed quickly, until the second hour arrived with less enthusiasm. "Do you know why we do night watch in twos?" Buck asked.

"No, sir."

"So we can talk and keep each other awake." Levi agreed while Buck continued. "What do you think of your first cattle drive?"

"I think it proves I'm still in search of what I am meant to do. But, I do like the experience of it. It sure beats the plow for weeks on end."

Buck adjusted in his saddle. "You never told me what it is you want to do."

"It's nothing that any farmer or rancher would want to hear. I'm trying to figure it out myself."

"Sometimes the best answer is a straight answer."

Levi waivered, hoping Buck would prove to be trustworthy. "I've heard of these schools you can go to after grade school. Instead of studying everything, you study what you want to be."

"Do you mean college?"

Levi looked at Buck in surprise. "Yeah."

"Why didn't you do that?"

"It wasn't my time. I needed to help my family. I felt that I needed to be there if they needed me."

"Was that because your paw left?"

"Yes, you could say that. He told me grade school was good enough. It was all I needed. All I ever wanted was to go to college. I never felt right with farming. I've always felt like there was something else inside of me. I listened to him and didn't go. And then he left. He left! I gave up my dream on his advice and he didn't even stay." Buck continued listening. "The day he left I stood next to him before he mounted his horse. My youngest brother, Matthew, was outside playing in front of us. He was running as fast as he could. I later realized Matthew was showing off for his paw and brother. I begged my paw not to leave. I pointed at Matthew and asked paw how he could leave his nine-year-old son." Levi restrained his gathering emotion. "Do you know what he said to me? He said that someday I would understand. He didn't even look me in the eyes." Levi breathed in steady anger. "I followed him to the end of our road and he told me to stop. I watched him ride away. Now you tell me, what is there to understand about any of that? How am I to understand leaving a nine-year-old boy? How do I understand leaving a wife, four children, and destroying a family? When does the day come that I understand any of that!"

Buck pulled the collar of his duster tightly around his neck. "How strong is your faith?"

"Do you mean in God?"

"Yes."

"It's strong. Strong enough, I guess. He's the only reason I have gotten through all of this."

"Do you think you have gotten through all of that?"

Levi looked into the stars again. "No."

"Then pray for *that* understanding. Pray for the day to come when you will have gotten through it all. And then you will know what it is that you are meant to do with your life."

The darkness cloaked Levi's tears. "Thank you." Levi pulled the rein and guided Arrow up the embankment. Buck watched him meander along the edge of the wash. Uneasy about Levi riding in the dark, he quelled his concern and allowed him time to confront his emotion. He thought of his own sons. His love for his family defined him. The blessings of his present life surpassed expectation. He hoped he had benefited Levi in some manner. He noticed the young man's harbored anguish and how it consumed him. Remembering the man he named Logan after, he felt it was his time to influence a soul. To benefit, to mentor, and to matter. What he would never want for his sons, he did not want for Levi either. Seeing his past abruptly face him at the Frederick train depot, he felt regret bombard his existence. The overwhelming desire to protect his present and future came with it. Just as a man named Logan saved him from himself long ago, he now felt compelled to do the same for Levi.

The sound of a running horse intensified as he looked about the area. Levi stopped Arrow at the edge of the wash and pointed toward the west. "Mr. Samson, over that way, I saw a campfire. And it's not ours."

Buck and Levi crawled underneath two mesquite trees and peered between the branches. The orange glow of a small fire highlighted the surroundings. The embers crackled and popped. They envied its emanating warmth. Buck surveyed the scene and saw that the wood was nearly burned to coals.

"I don't see anything," Levi observed.

Uncertain of the situation, Buck rose to a knee. "Something's not right."

"I know. Who leaves a fire burning without tending it?"

"Exactly. Let's get to our horses and ride to camp!"

"What's the matter?" Levi asked, running to keep up with Buck.

"An old scheme of cattle rustlers is to light a fire within sight of a herd to lure the cowhands away."

"So they can steal the herd?"

"Yes, and ambush the unsuspecting few left in camp." They reached their mounts and hurried toward Owen and the boys. "Levi, ride straight into camp. Look for Owen. If you don't see him, I want you to yell 'yee-haw' as loud as you can."

"Yes, sir." Buck rode westward. Levi guided Arrow down the embankment and into the campsite. He saw Owen standing around the fire with Logan and Daniel. "Is everything okay here?" Levi said as he dismounted. "We saw another campfire west of here." Owen stared at Levi without reply. Levi saw his eyes shift left in the bright firelight. He felt a sinking feeling hearing footsteps from behind.

"Hand over that revolver!" Levi turned to see a tall man aiming a gun at him. He untied the holster and handed it to the man. "Drop it on the ground and step over there with the others." Three more men stepped from the darkness.

"I thought you said there was a second man with him?" Another man asked.

"There was. You two go look for him. You stay with me." He knelt to pick up Levi's revolver.

Bam! The revolver jumped off the ground. The other men reached for their sidearms.

"Keep those heels holstered!" Buck's voice echoed across the wash.

The hostile men looked about the area. Owen bounded over the fire and dove for Levi's revolver. He rolled to his side and pulled the gun from the holster, aiming it into the face of the nearest man. "If any of your buddies move, you'll regret it."

"One at a time, take off your holsters, leave them on the ground, and step back. Starting with you!" *Bam!* Buck fired another shot from the darkness. The round exploded inches away from the farthest man's foot. He dropped his gun belt and held out his hands. Each of the four men followed Buck's demands. Owen gathered their weapons. "Boys, gather your things and mount up. Get to the herd!" Logan, Daniel, and Levi obeyed Buck's orders while Owen forced each man facedown in the dirt. "Over here," Buck called to Owen from the darkness. "Just slow them down, nothing more, you hear?"

"Sure." Owen handed Buck the guns. "Do you think Teague is out there?"

"I don't know. But we are getting out of here." Owen walked back to the men. He spun the revolver in his hand and held it by the barrel. "Sniff the soil, gentlemen!"

Buck watched Owen incapacitate the first man with a sharp blow to the back of his head. Buck traversed the slope. "Boys, where are you?"

"Over here, Pop," Daniel answered.

"We've got a few hours till sunrise. Make sure you have all of your winter wear on. It's going to be risky, but—Logan and Levi, go ahead and find a route for us. We're going to go as far as we can in the dark. There's a cattle crossing that runs east to west a few miles before we get to our land. We'll move the herd along that trail and then drive them north along the Deep Red Creek. That should keep whoever these men are from tracking us too easily. Once we get enough light to see, stay near the front of the herd and be ready to lead them at a quick pace. Logan, you know which direction is home, so do your best. You'll see that cattle crossing. If you run into any trouble, don't hesitate to use these." Buck handed them each a revolver. "Be careful, boys. Daniel, you come with me and we'll get Owen."

Logan and Levi rode along the edge of the wash. They found a gentle slope near the herd. They searched the area and galloped ahead to find a safe passage. The cold seemed to intensify with the darkness. The stars provided the only illumination, encouraging them to stay close together.

"Did you see that shot your father made? That was incredible!" Levi declared. "It hit right in front of that man's boot."

"Yeah, I can't believe it either," Logan replied.

"And Owen! I thought he was going to kill that guy."

"Yeah, I know."

"What's wrong with you?" Levi asked.

"I didn't know my father could shoot like that. I didn't even know he had a gun. I felt helpless when those men showed up. They took us by surprise."

"I know what you mean. I wish I had stood up to that guy. I handed him my gun like some scared child. That won't happen again."

"At least we have guns," Logan rested his hand on the holster.

"You have got to tell me about your father and Owen. They definitely appear to be more than they let on."

"I would like to know about them too. I thought I did."

Levi detected the resentment in Logan's voice. "You should be proud of your father. He is very brave."

"I'm not sure I know who he is. Why should I be proud of him when I had no idea about any of this?"

"What are you talking about? Good grief! Just talk to him."

"I was taken by surprise, that's all."

"Your father and Owen must have had an interesting past. I wonder how much Cole is involved with them."

"I don't know. Pop has hidden a lot from me and Daniel. I guess it finally came out tonight." Logan looked behind them. "I think we've gone far enough. Let's turn back. Pop will run these cows halfway to the headquarters if he decides too."

"Were those men back there cattle rustlers?" Levi asked.

"I guess so."

"I kept asking your father who was following us. He never answered me."

Logan stopped his horse. "I didn't even know anyone was following us. When did you find this out?"

Levi turned Arrow alongside Logan's mount. "I don't know why your father didn't tell you that or anything else. I've been riding with him because he told me to. In a way, I am his employee. So maybe he told me things because he wanted me to work a certain way."

"Or maybe he is protecting me and my brother," Logan countered. "I appreciate what you are trying to do, Levi. But like you said, I need to talk to Pop and ask him some questions I didn't know I had to ask." Logan looked ahead. "The land looks dark up there. It might be another wash. Let's head back." The boys lumbered toward the herd as six more men watched them depart from the wash ahead.

7

"Warren, let's rush them!"

Warren Teague and five men crouched along the edge of a wash. "Let them go. Go back and find out what happened to the men. Your campfire idea obviously didn't work."

"It has before," another man countered.

Warren exhaled in disgust. "You're trying to fool one of your own, you idiot. And your men were late."

"He's not one of us. He's the one that betrayed your brother."

Warren shoved his revolver into the holster. He walked toward the man and slammed his fist into his jaw. "You said you could handle this. It's taken me years to find him and this is what I can expect from you? I'm not paying you to tell me what I already know! Nothing has worked since we left Vernon. From now on I'll do the thinking. Get up!"

"What about the cattle?"

Warren backed away from the fallen man. "All in time."

"We're in this for the money *and* the cattle," a third man threatened.

Warren walked up the slope and looked down at the men. "And with my plan you'll get your cows, and maybe more when we get the man. Have some of your men follow them at dawn. He'd be crazy to move cattle at night. Track them for as long as it takes. Now go find out what happened to your men. And stoke that fire when you get there. I'm freezing."

"Maw, Mrs. Samson, they're here!" Rachel yelled through the door and ran to the wagon. Matthew climbed onboard with Ann and Beth hurrying to join them.

"They're heading to the pasture. We'll meet them at the fence when they drive them in," Cole Berenger directed from his horse. "Follow me."

They rode eagerly along the trail leading to the fenced pasture. The Deep Red Creek bordered the trail. The children pointed at their various play areas throughout the creek and told of their grand adventures. They enjoyed sliding down the steep banks and searching for freshwater mussels. Their stories became more elaborate the farther they rode.

"There! Right over there is where I found it," Matthew blurted.

"Where you found what?" Ann asked.

"This." Matthew reached out between the ladies and opened his hand. A large piece of flint rock covered his palm.

"That looks like an arrowhead. You found that in the creek?" Beth inquired.

"Yes, ma'am. Not far from where your land meets ours."

Ann looked at the jagged rock. "You should show that to Mr. Samson."

"I showed it to Mr. Bear. He said I should keep it for good luck or something."

"You really like Mr. Berenger, don't you?" Beth asked.

"Do we have to call him by his whole name?"

Beth held the reins with one hand and rubbed Matthew's cheek with the other. "You silly boy. As long as Mr. Berenger doesn't mind, you can call him what you want." Matthew smiled and sat near Rachel.

"You didn't tell them who showed you where to find that arrowhead," Rachel whispered.

"I know," Matthew replied. "I don't want Maw getting upset. Then she might not let us see him again."

Beth guided the horse team behind Cole on horseback ahead of them. "It's good to see the children take such a liking to Cole. I'm sure it is good for him too."

"It is nice," Ann replied.

"I'm sure they could use a father figure…" Beth hesitated. "I mean, oh, I'm sorry, Ann. I meant Cole could help them adjust." Beth's face flushed.

"I know what you meant." Cole motioned ahead and urged his horse into a faster gallop. Beth pointed through the woods. "Look! I see a whole lotta cows and some cowboys over there. They're bringing in the herd." She steered the wagon near the gate and watched Cole swing it open.

"Yee-haw!" Several of the boys waved at the women and children and drove the cattle through the narrow entry. The children cheered their arrival as Buck, Owen, Levi, Logan, and Daniel corralled the stray cows. Owen followed the remaining cows through the opening while Cole closed the gate. Buck, his boys, and Levi dismounted. Beth ran to Buck and united with a loving embrace. She kissed her boys and hugged them with a mother's love. Rachel and Matthew sprinted into Levi, knocking him down. They taunted their big brother. He fanned them away with his cowboy hat as Ann approached.

"Hello, Maw."

Ann saw his weathered appearance. Lines of dirt etched across his face. His tired eyes clashed with the happiness expressed in his smile. The battle against the winter wind chapped his skin. She noticed a newfound look of confidence in his hearty stance. "You look like a cowboy. Welcome home, son." They embraced with the children tugging at Levi.

"We've got a surprise to tell you." Matthew beckoned.

"Hold on, you two. I just got here. And I am so hungry I could eat my boots." Levi grabbed Matthew and hugged him. He then looked at Rachel. "How's my little sis doing?"

Rachel grabbed Levi's arm and nudged him. "You stink."

"Yeah! You smell like horse poop!" Matthew shouted.

"What? I think instead of a bath I'll just rub my stink off on you."

"No, you won't! I'll stick you with my arrowhead!" Matthew pointed the flint at Levi.

"Where did you get that?"

"The creek. My Indian friend showed me where to find it. Rachel got one too."

Levi took the arrowhead from Matthew. "Your Indian friend?"

Rachel shoved Matthew and whispered to Levi. "Yeah. He is really nice. But don't tell Maw. She will get upset."

Levi handed the flint back to Matthew. "Looks like you two have become quite the explorers. What else have you done while I was gone?"

"Open the gate!" Owen yelled, racing toward the gathering from the other side of the fence. His horse sprinted in full stride.

"What is he doing?" Cole asked and watched Owen circle the herd as fast as his horse could go. "Unlatch the gate for him!"

Logan and Daniel swung the gate wide. Owen charged through the opening and brought his horse to an abrupt stop. "Close it fast!" Owen demanded.

The boys pushed the gate closed. Everyone rushed to the fence. Buck saw the forty new cows scatter sporadically. Everyone heard the cattle bellow fearful cries and separate, leaving a clear passage through the center of the herd. Buck stared in astonishment. "Get away from the fence!" Buck drew his revolver and aimed at an enormous bison charging toward him. The huge beast careened through the cattle. The bison's lowered head and humped back powered through the herd with violent momentum. Buck pulled the hammer back as Matthew ran screaming.

"Don't shoot him!"

"Matthew, get away!" Buck yelled at Matthew pulling on his arm.

"He won't hurt us."

Buck yanked his arm away and aimed again. He placed his finger on the trigger and sighted between the animal's eyes. Matthew crawled under the fence in front of Buck.

"Matthew!" Ann screamed. Buck dropped his revolver and reached over the fence. The oncoming bison was ten yards away when Matthew turned around. Their eyes met in awareness of each other as Matthew reached out. He was suddenly lifted into the air and dropped on the other side. The bison reeled to a stop a few feet from the fence. Ann dashed to Matthew. "What were you thinking? You could have been killed."

"He wasn't going to hurt me."

"Don't you ever do that again, little boy!" Ann scolded.

Matthew looked at the bison. The animal towered over the fence, heaving air and observing everyone. Satisfied of the situation, the creature carelessly nibbled at the grass.

Cole walked next to Buck while Owen remained several yards away. Owen's horse meandered to the other side of the wagon and never looked back. The two men observed the bison. Buck picked up his revolver and kept it in hand. "Have you ever seen anything like that?" Cole asked.

"Which part?" Buck chuckled. "Where in the world did that thing come from?"

Cole scratched his head. "I think that explains the damaged fence I repaired a few days back. It was over on the east side."

"We're foolin' ourselves to think any fence we have will stop that animal. He could have barreled through this like it was yarn," Buck declared. He watched Matthew still being scolded by Ann and addressed him. "Young man, that was a foolish thing you did. That bison could have killed you."

Matthew wiped his eyes. "No, sir. You were going to kill it."

"Weren't you scared?"

"No, sir."

"Why not?"

"Because he is my friend."

Buck glanced at Ann and continued talking to Matthew. "Have you seen this bison before?"

"Yes. And it is a buffalo. He won't hurt you."

"How do you know that?"

Matthew looked over at Rachel standing nearby. "Because our Indian friend told him not to."

"Your Indian friend?" Buck asked.

"Matthew said the same thing to me," Levi interrupted and knelt next to his little brother. "Who is this Indian friend of yours, buddy?"

Crreak!

Everyone looked at the fence to see the bison nudge it. "He's scratching his back," Matthew explained. The group turned in bewildered unison at Matthew.

"I suppose he is," Buck agreed. "Listen, little fellow, let's make a deal. You promise me to never do that again and I'll let you ride Big G around the corral. Do we have a deal?"

"Yes, sir. I guess so."

"Good." He patted Matthew's head and winked at Ann. He walked away with Cole. Owen stood farther away from the fence. "So, we have a wild bison on our ranch."

"No, Mr. Samson," Buck and Cole heard Rachel say from behind them. "You have three."

The smell of cooked bacon blended with the aroma of fresh biscuits and simmering grits. Beth and Ann brought the breakfast items to the table.

Everyone found a seat. Cole and Owen thanked Buck and Beth for the welcomed invitation. Everyone raised their heads from the conclusion of the prayer and observed their first breakfast together in many days. Cole's completion of the chicken coop brought a lasting supply of eggs that were devoured within minutes. Matthew kept close watch for the sorghum and guarded his biscuit. The December wind howled outside while everyone enjoyed the bountiful meal, relieved that the cattle drive was over.

"At this morning's count, we have exactly eighty head of cattle and one bison," Cole announced.

"No, Mr. Bear. It's a buffalo, and there are three of them," Matthew corrected.

"Buffalo and bison are the same thing," Cole countered.

"Nuh uh. Buffalo are what we have. You have to call them buffalo."

"Did your Indian friend tell you that too?" Cole teased.

"Yes, he did. But he's my friend, not yours. You can't talk to him."

"Why not?"

"Because he doesn't like people that call them bison."

"All right, young man, that's enough. You don't talk to Mr. Berenger that way," Ann interjected. Matthew spanned a pompous smile toward Cole.

"I only let people that call them bison ride my horse," Cole refuted.

Matthew's smile quickly faded. "Oh yeah? Well, I'm gonna come over there and stick you with my arrowhead!"

"I'd like to see you try."

Matthew pulled the arrowhead from his pocket. His smile returned as he ran around the table toward Cole. "Hold your horses there, little buffalo. Let me see that." Buck sat Matthew on his lap and yanked the arrowhead from his hand. "Where did you get this?"

"Near the creek. I found it."

Buck studied the flint. "This looks big enough to have been on a spear. We need to go find the rest of the buffalo you and your sister keep talking about. On the way out, I want you to show me where you found this."

"My Indian friend showed me. Rachel and I both got one."

Buck handed the arrowhead to Matthew. "And who is this Indian friend you keep talking about?"

Rachel stepped near Buck. "He is very nice. He showed us the buffalo and even saved Matthew from the paw buffalo."

"You've seen him too?"

"Yes, sir."

"Where?"

"We only see him when we go on our land near our grandparents' graves."

"I guess it's that Wichita Indian, the one that helps animals." Buck noticed Ann taking a special interest in his words. "I haven't heard any concerns about him. He's a wanderer." He focused upon Rachel and Matthew. "You two be careful. The next time you see him, you come get me or one of the men, understand?" Both children agreed. "Let's get bundled up and go find those buffalo." The children applauded and ran to put on their winter clothing. Buck, his boys, Levi, and the children congregated on the wagon and headed down the path along the Deep Red Creek. They journeyed next to the water, talking about the cattle drive and the children's many adventures. Buck asked Levi to sit up front as the ruckus continued at the back of the wagon. "You did well on the cattle drive, Levi."

"Thanks for letting me go. Much obliged for the pay too. I haven't made that kind of money ever."

"With eighty cows, we are at capacity for the ranch and the farming areas. I will need to graze them on your maw's land. I'll pay her, and then we can get that lumber for your home."

"That sounds great. We're all excited."

"You know, Christmas is coming soon. I haven't heard any of you talking about it. I know money is tight, but is your maw planning anything for the children?"

"I doubt it. I heard her talking to Mrs. Samson about helping to pay for a Christmas Eve dinner, but I'm sure she hasn't planned anything else."

Matthew crawled to the front of the wagon. "I found my arrowhead up there by that bend in the creek. And look! There are the graves up there by those trees."

Buck parked above the creek. Rachel and Matthew led him to the site. The water level was low, exposing several extra feet of bank. Exploration filled the mind of each person. Rachel and Matthew pointed to the dirt where they had found their arrowheads. Buck sifted the earth with his hand. Fragments of flint were exposed an inch down. Buck and the children started digging with hopeful ambition. A widening circle began to deepen as they pushed the red earth from the area. Bits of mussel shells formed pockets in the ground.

"Look!" Rachel uncovered a smooth, heavy stone. Matthew dug in the same spot, uncovering a large piece of flint. The children handed the rocks to Buck.

"Do you know what these are? This rock was used to shape this flint. I'll bet whoever worked here sat on the edge of the creek, ate some mussels, and made the arrowhead you have from this piece of flint." Buck simulated banging the heavier rock across the flint. "You two may have found an Indian encampment. A long time ago, there were lots of them in this area. They lived here just like we do now. They probably had little children like you, running and playing around the banks of this creek."

"Where did they go?" Rachel asked.

"Some of them moved away. Others stayed here. Some still live in parts of Oklahoma."

"I like his clothes," Matthew said and kept digging.

"His clothes?" Buck questioned.

"My Indian friend has warm clothes. I like his hairy coat and his skin pants."

"His what?"

Rachel giggled. "He means his coat looks like buffalo hair and his pants look like animal skin. What do you call them?"

"Buckskin?"

"Yeah, that."

"His hair is longer than mine. I don't think I would want my hair that long. Look, I found another flint rock!" Matthew held up the stone.

"Where did you see this Indian?" Buck asked.

"Over there." Rachel pointed up the embankment. "He likes it here."

"How often do you see him?"

"Not much. He leaves when his friends arrive."

Buck looked up from the dirt. "There are others?"

"Yeah. But we never see them much. Our friend makes them leave with him."

Buck watched the children continue digging without regard to his uneasiness. "How many of them are there?"

"Pop! Over here." Buck stood at the sound of Logan's voice. He motioned for the children to follow. They rounded a large tree and saw

Logan and Daniel standing over several white bones partially uncovered in the mud. "We thought it was pieces of a calf or a deer until we saw that." Logan pointed at a round skull protruding from the earth.

Buck turned it with his boot. The bleached white skull showed red mud packed in the eye sockets. "This is human." Buck backed away. "And it's old. All of you get away from it. Let's not disturb it any more than we have. We'll round up some shovels and give whoever this was a proper burial when we come back."

"Who do you think it was, Pop?" Daniel asked.

"Son, out here, it could have been anyone—a cowboy on a cattle drive, a settler passing through, an outlaw, anyone."

"Or an Indian," Matthew added.

Buck looked at Matthew without reply. He motioned everyone up the rise to see Levi sitting near his grandparents' gravestones. "Boys, take the children on ahead. We'll catch up." He walked over to Levi. "Do you want some time, son?"

Levi remained focused upon the graves. "No. I realized I never said good-bye to them. They came up here for a new life and died for it. I miss Maw-Maw a lot. She held the family together. She was the heart of us all."

"Most grandmothers are."

"I still can't believe Paw-Paw was killed. Who could do something like that?"

Buck thought for words to benefit Levi's situation. "It's time for you to move on and make your grandparents proud. This is beautiful land and will make a nice farm, ranch, or whatever you and your maw decide to do. Concentrate on right now. That way you can pursue your schooling."

"I didn't see many colleges on our way into southwest Oklahoma."

Buck laughed. "True. But you never did tell me what you wanted to be if you did go to college."

Levi surrendered. "I want to be a writer."

"Nope, there's not many of those in southwest Oklahoma. So you should do well. You will probably be the first writer in this part of the state."

"I figured someone like you would think me foolish," Levi replied.

Buck faced the graves. "Look there at your kinfolk. Do you think them foolish? They left all they knew and came up here to pursue their dream. Do you call them foolish? No. The results are what they are. Foolish would have been them never pursuing their dream at all." Levi agreed without words. "Listen. Right now you're on Noah's ark, blowing in the wind without a sail. Give all of this to God." Buck touched Levi's chest. "Everything you have bottled up in there is ready to pop. And just like that ark, you'll reach the dry ground that He intends for you."

"I see why they call you the Deacon," Levi expressed.

"Now that title is a story for another time."

"Do you regret any of your past?"

"I regret only that which I have inflicted upon others. I have asked for forgiveness. I do my best to keep my faith and go on living a better life. It's all any of us can do."

"What if your past comes back to haunt you?"

Buck began to ponder Levi's purpose in asking that question. "We all have a past, son. The real trick is deciding to leave it there."

Levi took a last look at the graves and walked away with Buck. He drove the wagon near the fence on a small rise and dismounted. They crossed the fence and caught up with the others hiking through the pasture. The expansive land stretched in all directions. Except for Deep Red Creek and its outlying trees, there were few landmarks to identify the property line. The level terrain appeared to have no end. Buck spoke of plowed fields boasting plentiful harvests and rich grazing for their herd. The young men and children dreamed of better days as they listened to Buck's optimism. With every step, the next generation began to appreciate the property even more. Buck spoke with passion, eager to express his love for the land. A love that he hoped his young audience would someday have as much of.

They approached another rise as Matthew pointed to the horizon. "Are those clouds out there?"

"No. Those are the Wichita Mountains," Buck replied.

"Those must be big mountains to see them from here."

"They're big for the Great Plains."

"How far are they from here?" Matthew continued.

"I guess they're a couple of days on horseback. It depends on which way you go. They are very rocky. I've only seen them once, but they have these big boulders piled all over. Some of them are bigger than our house."

"Why do they call them the Wichita Mountains?"

"I think they named them for the Wichita Indians that lived there. They lived there long before any of us got here."

"Just like my Indian friend." Matthew smiled.

"I don't know about that. I think your Indian friend lives somewhere around here."

"I know he is glad the buffalo are safe in your fence," Matthew stated.

"He might be glad, but I'd be happier if they would leave my poor fence alone. And I don't want them hurting the cattle either."

"But you can't let them go. They are a family here."

"I was afraid of this." Buck stopped Matthew. "Bison, I mean, *buffalo* are very dangerous. They are wild animals. You saw what that big one tried to do to Mr. Tisdale. It nearly killed him and his horse."

"It was just protecting the maw and her baby."

"Maybe. But, if he tears the fence down again, all of the cows could get out and then we would be in big trouble."

Matthew frowned. "Can you please keep them in your fence for a little while? At least see them first."

"Are you sure there are three of them?" Buck asked, knowing it was hopeless to sway Matthew any further.

"Yes!" Matthew pulled Buck by his hand with renewed excitement. "Come on. The fence is over there. And see, it's not even broken. Let's go find them and I will show you." Matthew yelled for Rachel and crawled under the fence.

Everyone spread out to look for the buffalo. Several cows dotted the landscape grazing and roving peacefully. The late summer rains provided ample grasses for the winter. They traversed the area, seeing sections of the property they had taken for granted before. They reached another rise in the terrain and looked across the property.

"I don't see any buffalo out there," Buck exclaimed.

Rachel and Matthew searched with a juvenile's hope. Seeing nothing before them, they yearned for an explanation. "Let's keep going. They could be lying down. We might not be able to see them from here," Rachel proposed.

Buck grinned at her determination. "Come on, children. Let's get back to the wagon. If they are still inside the fence, then they must be on the other side of the woods. We'll try again another time." Rachel and Matthew reluctantly surrendered. The group followed the fence back to the waiting team. Buck checked the fence's condition. Levi considered a question he knew Buck had avoided earlier.

"Mr. Samson, whatever became of those men back on the cattle drive?"

"You asked earlier about the past coming back to haunt you." Levi nodded. "That may have been exactly what happened that night." He tugged on a section of fence and then approached Levi. "Those men were after our cattle. Our cattle are how we make a living. We protected the herd and got them here safely. That is all that matters. Be thankful no one had to die."

"Is that how it is in Oklahoma? Are we going to have to watch out for bad men like that?"

"No. There are good people here." Buck became hesitant. "There are things in my past that I do not want brought back. And I do not want them known to my wife, my sons, to you or to anyone. If it comes back to 'haunt me,' as you say, then I will do what I didn't do before and go from there."

"What would you do?" Levi asked.

"I would pray."

Buck and Levi moved to the wagon parked along the other side of the fence. The children, Logan, and Daniel enjoyed a longer route farther from Buck and Levi. They raced each other across the field to the wagon. Buck and Levi watched them sprint down a shallow depression from their elevated view. "I hope they don't spook those two cows over there," Levi stated.

Buck looked ahead of the children and his boys. "Those aren't cows!"

"What?"

"Children! Boys! Stop!" Buck bolted after them as they continued unaware toward two bison. The animals postured for confrontation. The children and boys sustained their oblivious contest. "Quit running!"

Logan saw his father waving frantically. He slowed his pace and glanced ahead. "Daniel, watch out!" The children looked back at Logan as the male bison charged. Buck reached the children and grabbed them. The bison accelerated toward the grouped targets. It rapidly covered the distance between them. Buck shoved the children to the ground. Several yards behind, Logan could only witness the bison's attack. He was preparing for the worst just as a larger object rushed across his view from the left. "Levi!"

The wagon team careened over the rise. The horses carved the soil with their powerful hooves and sliced through the air. The additional speed from the slope increased their forward momentum. Logan watched Levi angle the team's approach into the oncoming beast. The horses raced passed, perfectly timing the wagon's interference with the bison. The colossal brute hit the wagon broadside in a thunderous collision. The back wheels slid sideways from the impact, nearly flipping the wagon. Levi felt the wagon shift violently. He witnessed the bison stumble and veer away. He steered the team around and slowed them in front of the prone group. The bison glared at the wagon while Buck hustled the children and his boys onboard. Levi snapped the reins and guided the team safely away from the irritated animal.

"Is any one hurt?" Levi asked. The group clustered along the back of the wagon heaving with adrenaline. Levi observed his sister and brother for any injuries. Logan and Daniel watched the bison return to the female while Buck collapsed across the bed of the wagon.

"That was quick thinking, Levi," Buck said.

"Don't thank me just yet." Buck rose to see a sizeable section of demolished fence. "There wasn't a gate nearby, so I had to create one with the wagon."

They saw the two bison still watching them. "Matthew, Rachel, after what we just went through, your buffalo will have to find a new home. They are too wild to stay here." The children viewed the bison without a response. The horrifying ordeal churned within them, preventing any rebuttal. Buck calmed and observed the children's disappointment. "I know you like the buffalo. They seem to like it here, so maybe they will do better outside of the fence. Buffalo like to roam. And I thought you said there were three of them? I only see two, so maybe they can find the third one on the other side of the fence." Buck placed his arms around the children.

"They don't have to find it. It's hiding over there in the trees waiting for its maw," Matthew replied. Buck watched the female bison saunter toward the tree line.

Levi stood next to the bench. "What is that?"

Everyone observed the female bison obscure four lightly colored legs. The bison mother faced the attentive crowd, appearing to notice the intrigue upon her. The male bison positioned itself near the female, allowing a narrow passage between them. The wagon spectators watched as a well-developed baby bison hobbled between its parents. It stopped in full view of its audience and limped toward its mother. The children waved at the baby bison while the rest of the group stared in awe.

"Something is wrong with its leg," Rachel exclaimed.

"You see, I told you," Matthew said to Buck.

Buck gazed in disbelief. "Yes, you did. But, you didn't tell me it was a baby *white* bison." Buck, the boys and the children continued to observe the astounding sight.

Hidden deep within the trees, two men scrutinized the scene from their mounts. One man shifted his tobacco wad and spat on the ground. "That's him. Let's get back before dark." The two men tugged on their reins and rode quietly through the woods. Confident in their concealment, the two strangers never noticed Cole Berenger watching their departure from the creek.

8

The hearth fire burned brightly, highlighting every anxious face in the Samson homestead. The warm dinner added satisfaction to the barrage of storytelling conducted by the juniors. Everyone involved with the exploit of the day had their own version to tell. Each rendition became more expounded upon with heroes abounding from fading truth to convincing fiction. The women were the imprisoned audience that fueled the desire of each child to trump the previous narrator with a more dramatic account.

"You all had quite an adventure today," Ann Rowe commented. She rubbed her son's cheek with a mother's touch. "I'm just thankful you're in one piece. That bison must have been awfully mad at you."

"It was, Maw. It was going to run us over for sure!" Matthew said. "Levi drove the wagon team like a bullet, right in front of that buffalo. It smacked into the wagon so hard I thought it broke it in half!"

"That was quick thinking, son."

"Yes, it was," Buck agreed. "Even a second later and that bison would have sent us for a tumble."

"It was actually quite fun," Levi replied. "But, I thought it broke the wagon in half too!"

Buck centered his chair in the room. "Why didn't you two tell me that the baby is a white bison?"

"We thought all baby buffalo were white. Aren't they?" Rachel asked.

"No. A white bison is very, very rare."

"Have you ever seen one before?" Matthew asked.

"No. I don't know of anyone that has. I've only heard about white bison in stories from long ago."

"Didn't you say it looked injured?" Beth Samson joined in the conversation.

"Yeah! What should we do for it, Mr. Samson? It can't stay out there hurt. Can you help it?" Rachel pleaded.

"Now hold on, little lady. Helping injured cattle is one thing, but that bison is a wild animal. And even if it is a baby, it is dangerous trying to corral one at any size. You already saw what its maw and paw think about people getting near them. Besides, it is going to want to be around its maw. It still looks like it is feeding from her."

"We've got to do something for it," Matthew demanded.

Ann noticed the struggle on Buck's face. "Let's go children. You've bugged Mr. Samson long enough. We've had a big day, let's get to bed."

"But, Maw…" the children whined in unison.

"No buts, come on, it's bed time." Ann ushered the children away as they wished everyone a reluctant good-night.

"What are we going to do about those bison, Pop?" Logan asked.

Buck stared into the fire. "We're gonna leave them alone for now. I'll ask Jeb Moore at worship this Sunday. He raises horses in Elgin, Oklahoma, and he's coming down here to sell some this week. I remember him talking about bison awhile back. I'll see what he thinks." The door rattled from three firm knocks. All eyes focused upon the entryway. Logan opened the door and greeted Cole Berenger standing in the darkness. He acknowledged Logan through the brisk winter wind and glimpsed at Buck. The two men made eye contact for a second before Buck rose from his seat and faced Beth. "Honey, why don't you and the boys get on to bed? I'll be along shortly." He kissed Beth on the cheek and motioned for Cole to come near the fire.

Cole removed his gloves and rubbed his hands near the flames. Buck handed him a hot cup of coffee and returned to his chair. Cole sipped the beverage with gratitude and sat along the hearth. He removed his cowboy hat and kept his duster fastened about him, indicating his desire for a brief encounter.

"Good coffee." Buck nodded in reply. Cole set the cup on the hearth. "There were two of them, both on horseback. They followed the creek and saw you and the children when that bison attacked. You were right, they tracked the herd straight to us. It wouldn't have mattered if you had split the herd that night or sent for help. They would have found us here eventually."

"I'm not surprised," Buck responded.

"I am. Why wait until you are home to steal the herd when they could have rustled them on the open prairie during the drive?"

"They want more."

"More of what? Cattle?"

Buck rested his head against the chair. "Me."

Buck rubbed the last of the sleep from his eyes and finished buttoning his shirt. He rose from the bed and stretched his back, feeling the winter cold and his tiresome age stifle his Saturday morning. He approached the bedroom door hearing the muffled sound of children's laughter. He entered the living area welcoming the warmth of a roaring fire. The beckoning heat lured him to his rocking chair, tempting a postponed start to an expected day's work.

"Buck, come over here. You have to see this," Beth summoned from the window next to Ann.

Buck halted his momentum into the rocking chair and reluctantly addressed his wife. "I could sure use a few moments with this fire."

Beth frowned. "Would you get over here?"

"What are those young'uns going on about out there? I could hear their goofin' from the bedroom. The one day I can get some extra rest and they want to wake the roosters."

Beth grabbed his arm and pulled him to the window. "Stop your fussin'. Look!"

Buck greeted Ann and noticed her perplexity. She returned the greeting without facing him. "What has gotten you ladies all stirred up?" He looked out of the window at Rachel, Matthew, Levi, and his two boys. "Those little ones need to stay off the corral fencing. They could fall."

"You old goat, look again!" Beth demanded.

"Woman, if that fire burns out I'm gonna…" Buck blinked his eyes at the sight of a baby white bison trotting along the back of the corral. The anxious children cheered from the other side of the fence. They stretched their hands between the posts hoping to draw the bison with fresh hay. His sons kept pointing to the corner of the corral. Buck stepped in front of Beth, noticing a female bison watching the crowd. She stood motionless while the baby stepped gingerly about her. "Why are there two bison in my corral?"

"I don't know. The children didn't know either," Beth answered.

"Who put them in there?"

"Well, let's get some breakfast in you and then you can go find that out." Beth patted her husband on his chest and went into the kitchen.

"Ms. Rowe, if your children had anything to do with this, I'm gonna run them off my ranch with a hot poker."

"Mr. Samson, if they did, I just might help you."

Beth handed Buck a folded cloth napkin. "Here, take this biscuit with bacon and eat it on your way out. Ann and I want to know what's going on. I'll fetch your coat."

"You two are really enjoying this, aren't you?"

Ann tried to disguise her smile while Beth directed him out the door. "And don't you dare leave my napkin out there!"

"There had better be some hot coffee waiting for me when I get back!" Buck yelled.

"Mr. Samson! Come over here! You won't believe what we found!" the children exclaimed.

"I'm sure there's going to be a lot I won't believe," Buck scoffed. He approached the corral at the excited welcome of the children and his boys. He leaned against the post and stared at the two bison. "Anyone want to explain this?"

"Not us, Pop. We heard the children out here and came to see what they were yelling about. Then we saw the two bison," Daniel Samson declared. "We don't know how they got in there."

"Levi, what about you?" Buck asked.

Levi shrugged his shoulders. "Cole and Owen are still in the cabin asleep. None of us heard or saw anything. I came out here to quiet the children and saw the two bison in the corral."

Buck looked around the corral. "Any sight of the bull bison?"

All of the younger folk became still. "We didn't think of that, Pop," Logan Samson responded. Everyone surveyed the area, remembering their previous encounter with the fierce bison.

Buck watched the baby bison walk to the center of the corral. "Is that a bandage on its leg?"

"Yes, it must have hurt itself on the fence or something," Rachel said.

"I can see that it got injured. But what concerns me, young lady, is who put the bandage on its leg?"

Buck noticed Matthew stepping slowly away from the conversation. "Matthew, can you help your sister with answering my question?"

"Do I have to?"

Buck glared at Matthew. Levi hurried next to his brother. "Matthew, don't talk to Mr. Samson that way! Answer him."

"I don't know what to say!" Matthew shouted. "Rachel and I promised each other we would not say anything. He just wants us to take care of the little buffalo until it gets better."

"Who wants you to take care of the buffalo?" Levi asked.

"Maw will get mad at us again if I tell you."

"She will get even more upset if you don't."

"I didn't mean for you to break any promise," Buck intervened. "Don't you remember how frightening it was when that big buffalo charged at us? That bull could have hurt all of us very badly, and that little buffalo could hurt you and your sister too. Don't you two ever touch that buffalo again without me, do you understand?"

"But we didn't touch it. Our Indian friend put the bandage on its leg. He wanted the baby buffalo to stay in your corral until it healed," Rachel announced, breaking her promise with Matthew.

"Can he stay? Please?" Matthew begged.

Buck stood with mounting frustration. "Where is your Indian friend?"

"He's gone. He never stays long," Rachel said.

"Boys, go check the barn. Look in every corner for anyone that might be hiding in there," Buck directed. He watched his boys sprint toward the barn, narrowly missing Cole and Owen walking by. Buck spied the surrounding area for anyone around.

"Good morning, Deacon," Owen greeted. "Everyone seems eager for an early start today." Owen saw Cole staring ahead and looked in the same direction. "What in the world is that? Is that what I think it is?"

"It is," Buck replied. "I guess that rules out any chance you two let those bison in the corral last night?"

Owen shook his head while Cole continued staring at the white buffalo and its mother. "Who doctored its leg?" Cole asked.

"Apparently, the children have an Indian friend that favors bison. I think it's that Wichita Indian that wanders these parts. The one all the stories are about," Buck answered reluctantly.

"Does this Indian friend have free reign of the ranch too?" Cole jabbed.

"That's just my point. You two keep a close eye out for any intruders or folks we don't know," Buck advised.

"I'll get rid of the bison after breakfast," Cole stated.

"No, Mr. Bear Ranger! You can't do that. Little Ghost needs to stay here with its maw and get better. It's what our Indian friend wants," Matthew said.

"I don't care what your friend wants. Those animals are wild and don't need to be here."

"That's right, children," Buck joined in. "We need to get them out of here, especially before you grow fond of them."

"Oh, we already have," Matthew announced. "Its name is Ghost, because it's special."

"No, it isn't. I told you to stop calling it that. I don't like that name, do you, Mr. Samson?" Rachel turned confidently toward Buck. "A ghost means it is dead. It's too special for a name like that."

"Maybe you shouldn't name it then," Buck said.

Rachel watched the little bison bounce and play in the center of the corral. "It sure is a happy little thing."

"Yep, it does have spirit," Cole said.

"Yeah, that's it. I'll name it Spirit. Thanks, Mr. Berenger. I like that. Everyone has a spirit, because spirits are alive."

"Very good, Cole. Why not name the mother while you're at it," Buck taunted.

"I didn't do anything! She's the one that named it!"

"Our Indian friend would like that name too," Rachel added.

"This Indian friend of yours sure seems to know his stuff," Owen chuckled and walked back to his cabin for breakfast.

Cole watched the baby bison. "In all my days, I have never seen a live white bison before. I think the hide of a white one is worth a lot of money. I'll watch for any strangers. We should probably start some checks around the fence line to make sure. I'll do some rounds after I count the cattle today."

Cole departed for the cabin with Rachel waving good-bye in gratitude. The small animal's eyes contrasted boldly against its curly, vanilla fur. Its protruding nose and simple expression amplified its cuteness to the admiring children. The female bison appeared more relaxed with the constant attention from the onlookers. She seemed to enjoy the humans gloating over her baby. The baby bison sunk its hooves into the soil and pranced about the corral, still favoring his wounded leg, but staying within sight of his mother.

Rachel and Matthew surrounded Buck with hope in their eyes. Rachel poured on the charm and questioned Buck. "Don't you like the baby buffalo, Mr. Samson?"

"Its name is Spirit, huh?" Buck dreaded the next unsaid question that he knew would require an agreement. Remembering his breakfast that still awaited, he avoided the pending spat altogether. "They can stay for a little while." Both children cheered. "But, don't get too used to them. Like it or not, they will need to find a new home once that little one is healed." The children agreed to every demand, forgetting each one with every step Buck took back to the house.

Several horse-drawn wagons lined the front of the headquarters. The December wind howled in varied gusts, reminding of winter's approach. The sun provided a perception of heat through the cloudless sky. The crisp Sunday morning hinted at the anticipation of Christmas for all those assembled for worship in the Samson home. Smoke billowed from the stone chimney, indicating an inviting fire. The believers congregated in prayer, thankful for the heat, food, and fellowship within the walls of the sturdy dwelling.

The breeze tossed a mixture of grass and leaves against the window, distracting Matthew from the prayer. His nine-year-old attention span strayed from Buck's sermon to the excitement of the bison waiting in the corral. He peeked at the many occupants around the room. Neighboring ranchers and farmers unified their faith with understanding and willingness. Several families gathered to establish their residence and join in support of each other's needs. Assistance with building a barn, wiring a fence, and starting a new school were a few topics of the gathering. Matthew noticed a new family sitting near the window. The husband and wife sat closely with their two daughters. Matthew was fascinated at the sight of their brilliant blond hair that flowed along either side of the girls' faces.

"Matthew!" Ann whispered. Matthew shut his eyes. He waited for the one word he knew for every prayer.

"Amen," the group concluded.

Buck stood with a welcoming smile. "Thank you all for worshipping together today. Make sure you meet our guests from Elgin—Jeb and Janet Moore, and their daughters, Mariah and Meredith. Jeb is a horse rancher down here looking for business. So, if any of you are in the market for a horse, come see him."

The door flew open unexpectedly, revealing a stranger's silhouette. His large cowboy hat and black high-collared duster prevented anyone from recognizing him. He raised his head, revealing his squinted eyes and unshaven face. "My apology for the interruption, but I heard there is a church service that meets here?"

"Yes sir, there sure is. Welcome! Come in and have a seat. We were just about to start the second part of our meeting—the food," Buck said. "I'm Buck Samson and this is my wife, Beth."

"Name's Smith."

"You're just in time, Mr. Smith. Please join us," Beth invited.

"Much obliged, ma'am." Mr. Smith stayed along the wall. He watched the gathering make their way to the kitchen. He surveyed the room with eyes that remained shaded under his cowboy hat. No one seemed to notice his observation until he saw Cole glaring at him from the opposite corner.

"This was a great worship service, Buck. It is always a pleasure to get down here and fellowship. Too bad Elgin isn't on this side of the Wichita Mountains," Jeb Moore said.

Buck turned from watching Mr. Smith. "It's always good to see you, Jeb. And it's about time you brought the family. You all need to visit more often."

"Maybe if you would buy a horse from me every month, I'd take you up on that! Listen, do you think we could take a look at that bison you mentioned? I'm dying to see it."

The two men strolled out to the corral with Rachel, Matthew, Logan, and Daniel in tow. They stopped at the fence and whistled for the bison. Buck pointed to the corner of the corral at the bison cow seated comfortably on the ground. "It's around here somewhere," he stated.

"Spirit, where are you?" Matthew shouted. At once, the children saw a furry, white face with big eyes and a wet nose pop up from behind the female. The children waved with unbridled enthusiasm. "He knows his name!" Matthew declared.

The little bison sauntered in front of its mother. "You're right, that's a white bison. Amazing," Jeb said. "Where's the father?"

"We don't know. But you don't want to tangle with him. He's a feisty one. And big," Buck replied.

"You know, the Indians hold the white bison in high regard. It even holds a spiritual significance. You gave him a good name."

"That's nice, but I need to get rid of both of them," Buck whispered to avoid Rachel and Matthew overhearing.

"Mr. Samson, you said we could keep them!" Rachel announced from behind him. Matthew ran between the two men, waiting for the conversation to proceed.

Jeb chuckled at the children. "I see your dilemma." He knelt beside the children. "Did you know there are bison just like yours living in the Wichita Mountains?" The children listened. "About three years ago, President Roosevelt set up a game preserve in the mountains for certain kinds of animals. They brought in some bison from a zoo in New York on a big train so they could live in the mountains again."

"Do they have a white one like us?" Matthew asked.

"I doubt it," Jeb replied. He addressed Buck away from the children. "It might be off the subject, but a white bison is extremely rare. I'm sure a number of folks back east would pay a lot of money for that little guy. It's just something to think about, if you want to get rid of it and get some compensation for your effort."

"If it's worth a lot, then any amount would go a long way to helping out this family. Those two children found it. They've been living with us until they can get on their feet. The right amount of money could certainly help get a house started for them."

"Let me know and I can ask around for you."

"Thanks, Jeb."

"Is that a white bison you have in there?"

Buck and Jeb turned around to see Mr. Smith standing nearby. Buck looked toward the house to see Cole leaning against the wall watching Mr. Smith. He observed Cole's distinctive stance attempting to hide his holstered revolver. He shifted his attention back upon Mr. Smith. "We're not sure what it is. I think we should all get back inside and enjoy that fine meal." Buck extended his arms and urged everyone toward the house. "Logan, Daniel, round up the children and let's go eat."

Mr. Smith did not move. "What? I bet you half a herd of buffalo hides that little feller is a white bison."

Logan revealed a startled expression. Buck noticed his abrupt posture. "Son, what's wrong?" Logan watched as Mr. Smith noticed him. Buck saw the staring match between them and interfered. "Mr. Smith, I think we should get going."

Mr. Smith raised his head with a defiant tone. He adjusted his duster along the belt line and took a step backward, unknowingly nudging someone. He spun around to see Cole next to him.

"The man said it's time to go," Cole warned with his arms crossed, fully exposing the heel of his holstered revolver.

"I heard him."

"Then get movin'."

Mr. Smith acknowledged with an insolent smile. "Thank you for your hospitality, Mr. Samson. You folks have a fine day." He addressed Buck and Jeb and stared at Cole. The two men stood as if they were daring each other to draw. Mr. Smith tapped his hip revealing the sound of a strapped revolver hidden beneath his duster. His smile deteriorated. He stepped to the side and walked passed Cole. Cole watched him mount his horse and ride south.

"Son, what happened to you?" Buck asked.

Logan motioned for Buck to walk with him as Cole joined them. "Do you remember when I found that man dying near the creek, the man that was shot?"

"Do you mean Levi's grandfather?" Buck asked.

"Yes. Before he died, he told me as much as he could about the man that shot him. And, I remember him saying the man said, 'I bet you half a herd of buffalo hides,' to him before he shot him."

"Are you sure?"

"Yes, I couldn't forget something like that."

"Why?" Cole interjected.

"Because he died next to me after he said it."

Buck consoled Logan. "Why didn't you tell me this before?"

"I didn't think it mattered until now."

"I'll bet you half a herd of anything that guy is trouble," Cole stated. "He's probably one of those men that tracked us the other day. And I'll bet the other half that his name is not Smith."

Buck agreed. "Cole, go get some food and get warm. I need to talk with Logan. Stash your sidearm before you go in, please. And Cole—thanks." Cole patted Logan on the back and walked away. Buck motioned Logan toward the fence. "Did their grandfather say anything else to you?"

"Nothing that I can remember. He mentioned some men riding up and talking to him. One man said those words and then shot him. That's when Daniel and I left to find you, after their grandfather died next to me."

"You did the right thing." Buck searched to find a means of comfort for Logan. "I'll find the right time to discuss this with Ms. Rowe. Until then, I think it would be wise to keep this between us. That poor family has been through enough."

"Pop." Logan looked at Spirit playing in the corral. "Why was Mr. Berenger carrying a revolver?"

"He probably shouldn't have done that. It's nothing that your mother or brother need to know about? You forget about that and let's go get you warm."

"Is it because he was a gunman?"

"What would make you say that?"

Logan became angry. "Were you a gunman?"

"What?" Buck said. "What are you talking about? Nothing you are saying has anything to do with—"

"Were you!" Logan shouted.

"We are not talking about this."

"Oh." Logan began to walk away. "I'll go find Levi. I'm sure you would talk to *him*." Logan continued toward the house.

Buck watched him leave. The day he dreaded since the birth of his oldest son had arrived. Hoping time and distance would erase his fear only delayed what was inevitable. He leaned against the corral fencing and realized his past was now infiltrating his present life. The stress of guilt and shame crept back into him. Logan crippled his confidence and left him searching for what to do. He clasped his hands together against the fencing and lowered his head between his arms. "God, please help me. Help me be a good father. Tell me what to say to him."

"Are you talking to the ground?"

Buck rose from his prayer to see Owen in the corral. "It might appear that way."

"I guess that's okay, as long as the ground doesn't answer!" Owen dropped a feed bucket near Buck's feet. "Sure is starting to look like the old days around here."

"What makes you say that?" Buck inquired with a firm tone.

"I haven't seen Cole square off with anyone like that since…well, you know."

"No, I don't know! So why don't you get your feeding done and come inside. I've had about enough of this recollection of the past from all of you."

Owen stepped in front of Buck. "Hold your horses there, Deacon. You may be the boss around here, but don't you go thinkin' you can bottle up your past and then let it spew all over me. You can stand here and pray till you're blue in the face. But it ain't gonna change a thing until you face what you said."

"And what's that?"

Owen placed his boot on the bottom fencing. "Be a good father and say what you should. Go talk to your son."

Buck looked into the sky, watching a red-tailed hawk circle nearby. "You don't know how much I have dreaded this moment—to see my past in the eyes of that Mr. Smith, to see another threat from some stranger, and to see another problem get solved with a bullet. I look back on it and for the life of me none of those bullets ever solved anything." Buck kicked the dirt. "I came here to get away from that life. You, Cole, and I all wanted what we saw others had. We wanted peace, remember? A quiet life without having to look behind us everywhere we went. I wanted to settle down. Now, we have all of that only to see the past walk up with the same kind of face, with the same threatening look, carrying another gun at the ready." Buck looked at Owen. "I hate my past. It took me years to get it behind me. That is not who I am anymore. That's why I don't want my family to know."

"True. But then your family will never really know you."

"I don't want them to."

"That may be, Deacon. But that's not your choice anymore, is it? You had your son standing right in front of you asking about his father. He doesn't care about your past or what you did in some forgotten Arizona town. He wants to know who his father is. You owe him that."

Buck considered this without resolve. The feelings for his son and his family clashed with the uncertainty of the day's events. He felt demoralized from the failed conversation with Logan and the resurrection of his earlier life. "I don't know that I can."

Owen picked up his bucket. The anguish on his friend's face tore at him. "Then that is what you should pray for. Pray for strength. We both know you have the words. You just need to let them out."

"Owen, you and Cole keep watch for any strangers around here, especially that Mr. Smith. If Logan is right, that might be the man that killed the Rowe family's grandfather."

"Are we just going to stand here and let them keep spying on us? You know they are here. It's only a matter of time, if that truly is the guy that killed him."

"We don't know that. And I don't want to risk anything with these families. Hopefully, they will leave us alone and move on," Buck countered.

"It's one thing to hope, Deacon. But it's quite another to be naïve."

"Hope is what I have turned to. Not the gun. And so have you." Buck looked at the distant pasture. "Keep a good count of the cattle too."

Owen observed the strain on Buck's face. Realizing any further discussion was in vain, he surrendered to his friend's yearning. "Sure thing, boss."

Buck watched Owen depart with harbored frustration. The smell of burning mesquite and leaves scented the air, turning his attention to the threat of fire. He hurried around the corral to locate the source of the smell. White smoke rose from a section of trees behind the house. He ran to see the children, Ann, and Beth gathered around a small fire with their church friends. Relieved from imagining the worst, Buck approached the fire surrounded by smiling faces trying to stay warm.

"I was wondering where you were," Beth said. "Logan seemed upset. But he wouldn't talk about it. What's wrong?"

"Everything's wrong," Buck snapped. Beth watched him curiously. Buck acknowledged the gathering and stepped next to Ann, Rachel, and Matthew. "Ms. Rowe, children, we need to talk." He ushered them away from the huddled group. Beth observed his odd demeanor and moved closer. The mixed emotions of frustration and panic depicted a combination she had not seen in him before. "I was talking to Mr. Moore about Spirit and I think I may have found a way to get you started on your house." Ann and the children listened attentively. "Mr. Moore knows some people that would pay a lot of money for Spirit. And like I said, to help you get started on your house, I would give you all the money we could get."

Ann placed her hand over her mouth. "Mr. Samson, that is too generous of you. Whatever you can spare, we would be grateful to you."

"Why do people want to pay money to see Spirit?" Rachel asked. "They could come here for free."

Ann looked at her daughter. "No, honey. Mr. Samson means he would sell Spirit and whoever bought him would take Spirit away to live with them. He would have a new home with people that would take care of him."

"No!" Matthew shouted.

Anticipating the reaction, Buck revealed his weakened restraint. "I have tried to tell you and your sister that having wild bison on the ranch is dangerous. I can't have them damaging my fences and eating the grass meant for the cattle. I need you both to think about your maw. This money would go a long way to getting your own home." Buck paused. "I'll make the arrangements. Besides, you've got to be tired of sleeping on that hard floor of mine. And it's gotten to where you can't hear yourself think in the house anymore."

"Oh. I'm so sorry." Ann's faced flushed at Buck's declaration.

Buck realized his comment. "Uh, no, Ms. Rowe, that's not what I meant. I meant to say that, um…"

"What Mr. Samson meant to say was that we want you all as comfortable as possible and that you are welcome to stay with us as long as you need," Beth interrupted. "Now why don't we all go back to the fire and warm up. Our friends are leaving and we need to see them off." Beth glanced at Buck with a firm expression.

"Are you taking Spirit away?" Matthew asked Buck.

"Yes, son, he is," Ann intervened. "Mr. Samson is trying to help us."

"Are you taking his maw too?" Rachel questioned softly. "Will they be together?" Buck watched them walk away without providing a reply.

"I don't want his help anymore," Matthew muttered to Rachel.

"Watch your mouth, little boy! You apologize to Mr. Samson this instant!" Ann demanded.

"That's not necessary," Beth comforted. "They're upset. Come now. Let's get warm." Beth shuffled them away and whispered to Buck, "What has gotten in to you?" She stood for a moment and then left for the fire.

"Beth." Buck saw Logan exit the house and mount his horse. Logan noticed Buck and then rode off with Owen. Buck watched his son disappear beyond the woods. He then focused upon the children. Both of their heads were low as they sat quietly near the fire. Turmoil churned within him. He contemplated his actions moving contrary to his emotions. He walked toward the house avoiding the departing guests and entered the vacant dwelling. He ignored the depleted lunch items and collapsed into his rocking chair with longing thought.

9

The darkness closed in behind Rachel, urging her to run faster. Ahead, little Spirit bellowed a frightened call to its mother. The bison cow joined with her baby and hurried away toward the light. Rachel screamed without sound for the bison to hasten their pace. She looked back to see the darkness appear as dense fog engulfing everything in its path. The obscure clouds parted for a moment, allowing several black horses to race through the opening. They galloped with a sinister presence. Their long, ebony manes flowed in the squall with each surge of their approach. The stallions raised their heads in unison, revealing fiery red eyes that scorched the darkness. Rachel shrieked in vain and turned toward the slowing bison. She struggled to form words through her anxiety. A sense of hopelessness slithered within her as she noticed the light shining brightly along the path ahead. The heated breath of the ominous steeds burned at her back while the darkness surrounded her. She felt her maturing determination encounter a quandary that her experience could not defend against. Fear turned to panic as she concentrated ahead of her. Expanding in clarity, Rachel observed the distinct outline of boulder-strewn mountains along the brightened horizon.

The light began to fade as the darkness wrapped around her tiring stride. The two bison bellowed their distress across the endless plains. The black fog enveloped her, halting her fleeing stride. A shimmer of light pierced the heads of the horses while they bore down upon her. Faceless riders appeared upon their backs and pulled on the lightning reins of each devilish horse. They remained at a tempting distance from Rachel, avoiding the light. Rachel shielded her eyes and faced the light. She screamed at the sight of a glistening human skull hovering behind her. Blinding light beamed from the eye sockets that turned toward the rock-covered mountains. The skull faced Rachel, revealing a skeletal body that glowed in the darkness. It raised its bony finger while staring at Rachel. Suddenly, the horses charged as the skeleton pointed abruptly toward the mountains. The horses' eyes resembled red-hot coals fueling their powerful approach. She ran toward the mountains and stumbled across the ground. She raised her head from the dirt and saw the two bison standing nearby. The earth trembled from the circling horses as the faceless riders raised their rifles and took aim at the bison. Menacing laughs echoed across the darkened plains as the riders pulled their triggers.

"No!" Rachel jumped from her bedding. Firelight flickered across the wooden walls of the room. Beads of sweat rolled down her forehead. She collected her thoughts and stood on her blankets bunched over the floor. She fixated upon a shadow passing across the firelight. *I am awake*, she reminded herself and felt the fear suddenly become reality. She stepped slowly into the main area of the house. The flames tossed vibrantly from the fireplace, highlighting a figure facing the window. "Matthew?" Rachel whispered. The figure didn't move. Rachel stepped closer, causing the floor to creak.

"Shh!" Matthew demanded.

"Why didn't you answer me? What are you doing up so early?"

"I had a bad dream."

"So did I. I had a scary one. What are you looking at?"

"Him."

Rachel felt the back of her neck tingle. She watched Matthew point at the window. She leaned closer. The fire highlighted a large man's face with his eyes appearing inches from the darkened window. "Ah!" Rachel covered her mouth.

"Don't scream, you'll scare him," Matthew scolded.

Rachel noticed his long, black hair against each side of his face. "What does he want?"

"He wants us to come outside."

Jeb Moore jumped from his wagon and approached the Samson household. His wife waited on the wagon while his two daughters ran to the corral. Their long, blond hair wisped in the morning chill, struggling for conformity against the ruffling movement of their anxious strides. Jeb pounded on the door to be met by Buck. The two men exchanged greetings and walked toward the corral. Buck buttoned his overcoat and shivered in the cold air.

"I guess you changed your mind about the bison?" Buck asked.

"I got to thinking about it. I guess if I had the animal with me it would be more convincing and more likely to get it sold for a better price," Jeb responded. "That and with Christmas a few days away, buyers might be plentiful."

Buck adjusted his cowboy hat and noticed the girls approaching them from the corral. "Christmas isn't the best timing for this around here, but you're right. Are you taking them both?"

"No, just the white one. Did you ever find the bull bison?"

"It disappeared. Haven't seen it for a while now," Buck replied. Buck turned his attention to Mariah and Meredith. "My goodness, if you two aren't the prettiest young ladies in southwest Oklahoma!"

The girls grinned with photogenic modesty. "Mr. Samson, did you move the bison into your barn?" Mariah asked.

"No, they are in the corral."

"The corral is empty," Meredith answered. "We didn't see anything."

The group reached the corral. "Was the gate open when you got here?" Buck asked the girls. They shook their heads. "Cole, Owen, are you in there?" Buck yelled toward the cabin.

Levi opened the door, followed out by Cole and Owen. "Good morning, Deacon. What's the ruckus this morning," Owen asked and greeted the visitors.

"Any idea where our two bison are?"

"Levi!" Ann shouted from the house. "You all come inside for breakfast. Tell Rachel and Matthew to come in too."

"Yes, Maw. I guess I have to find my sister and brother. I'll see if they might know where the bison are. They are out here with them every morning."

"Deacon, Levi, come over here." Cole motioned toward the cabin. He pointed at some chalk scribbled across the outside wall. "What do you make of that?"

The entire group gathered near the wall and read the elementary writing. The chalk pieces rested on the ground underneath the inscription.

Levi read the words aloud: "Took the buffalos to the mountains. They will be safe. Tell Maw do not be mad."

"Oh great," Buck mumbled. "Didn't any of you hear them? How in the world could two children have gotten two bison from this corral without any of you hearing them? For Pete's sake! You live right by the corral! Levi? You didn't hear anything last night? Your own kin waltz in here and take two bison right from under your nose and not one of you hear a thing? Those young'uns are more trouble than they're worth!"

"Buck Samson!" Beth announced from behind the group. Buck turned to see Ann standing next to her.

Ann walked through everyone toward Levi and glanced at the writing. "Where are they?"

"I don't know, Maw."

"I'm afraid I do," Jeb Moore said. "They may be heading for the Wichita Mountains. They heard me talking about the bison they have there. It's a game preserve. They may be taking them there."

Ann composed herself and faced Jeb. "Mr. Moore, how far away are those mountains?"

"Well, ma'am, if they're on horseback…"

"They are," Cole interrupted. "Two of our horses are missing in the barn."

Buck kicked the dirt. Beth grabbed his arm. "Buck, that's enough."

"They're children. And if they truly are driving those bison to the Wichita Mountains, they probably have several hours head start on us."

"Deacon, I've got this one." Cole then addressed Ann. "I'll get them, ma'am. It shouldn't be too hard to track them. They're going north."

"I'm going too." Levi grabbed his mother's hand. "They can't be too far."

"Thank you, Mr. Berenger." Ann smiled at Cole and Levi and turned toward Buck. "I do apologize for the behavior of my children. You and Beth have been too kind for so long. When my children return, we will be leaving." Ann departed toward the house. Beth released her husband's arm and pursued Ann.

Cole and Levi entered the cabin and grabbed their winter gear. "I'll get your mounts ready," Owen stated. "I'll pack some food and extra blankets too. Mr. Moore said there's word of a winter storm brewing in the Texas panhandle, so bundle up."

Cole stood over his wooden chest. He pulled two revolvers and a rifle from the trunk. He checked one of the revolvers and extended it toward Levi. "You might need this. Be careful with it."

Levi reached under his bed and held up his uncle's rifle. "I'll be fine." Levi continued packing. Cole lowered his arm as a slight smile crept across his face. The two men carried their packs and rifles to their waiting horses and mounted. Cole acknowledged Buck and turned his horse northward with Levi in close pursuit. Owen watched them race away and joined Buck.

"I'm really sorry about this, Buck," Jeb stated.

"It's nothing you did. These children need discipline. I know they're just being children, but this is uncalled for." Buck looked back at Owen staring into the trees. "Jeb, get your family and join us for breakfast. It doesn't look like we will be taking advantage of any Christmas buyers this year." Jeb thanked Buck and walked toward the house. Buck turned to see Owen sprinting toward him.

"Deacon! Get down!" Owen slammed Buck against the ground as the distinctive whine of a bullet raced above them.

Jeb looked into the direction of the gunshot. Buck rolled onto his side and crawled near a corral fence post with Owen prone behind him. "Jeb, get on the ground!" He watched Jeb run toward the house as another shot burst from the trees. The dirt in front of Jeb exploded in a cloud of dust. He dove onto the ground and rolled near the door. The door opened to Jeb's relief as he sat up to crawl inside. The muzzle of a rifle met him between the eyes.

"Come in, Mr. Moore." Jeb saw Warren Teague staring down at him. Another man grabbed Jeb by his shirt and threw him onto the floor near his family. "Please, join us. It may not be church, but you will have something to pray for shortly." Jeb held his daughters close with his wife nearby. Six gunmen stood at the ready inside the house. Beth and Ann stood together with Logan and Daniel near the bedroom. Warren yelled out of the door and aimed his revolver at Buck. "It seems we have you in a cross fire, Mr. Samson. So, why don't you be the brave man that you are and quit hiding behind that fence post?" Warren aimed at the post and fired. The bullet shattered the top of the post, raining pieces of wood upon Buck. Another shot followed from the woods, splintering the post in half. "Let's go, Buck. I'm not going to let a piece of wood take my glory." Warren stepped from the door and aimed again.

"Are you taking the coward's way?" Buck hollered.

Warren's expression tightened. "Call me that again, you haughty fool. Get off the ground and face me!"

"At least your brother knew what a fair fight was. I saw him in the eyes, unlike you, you coward." Warren fired multiple times at the fence post until only two feet of wood remained. His revolver clicked from empty rounds as he kept firing. "Now, Owen! He's out!" Buck urged. Buck and Owen crouched low and ran for the cabin.

Shots erupted from the trees, whizzing past them as they pushed through the door. "Don't shoot Samson! Leave him for me," Warren yelled toward the trees and then pointed into the house. "Three of you get down there and surround that cabin!"

"They probably have guns in there," one of the men warned.

Warren contemplated. "Get some torches and burn them out. Hurry!"

Three of the men rushed out of the room. The last man tripped over Mariah's leg as she leaned next to her father, crashing into the wall. Beth glanced at Logan and motioned toward the bedroom. "Look under the bed," she whispered. She stared desperately at her son with a mother's love, uncertain of her spontaneous action. The three remaining men taunted the fallen man and helped him up. With their backs turned, Logan slipped into the bedroom and closed the door halfway.

Warren and the three gunmen were joined by the two snipers from the trees. They surrounded the cabin and lit makeshift torches with hay, rope, and pieces of wood from the barn. "Watch the windows. If they do have guns, they'll be firing from there," one of the gunmen warned.

Owen peered from the back of the cabin through the window. "Any ideas? All I have is my revolver and my rifle in the corner."

Buck sniffed the air. "I smell smoke."

"Get out of the way, Deacon. I'll reduce their numbers as best I can." Owen cocked his revolver.

"Watch out!" Buck shouted as several large pieces of burning lumber crashed through the windows and door. One of the torches hit a bed, igniting it instantly. Smoke began to fill the room as more torches careened into the back wall. Both men began to cough as the situation worsened. "Owen, it's me they want. Once I'm gone they'll go for the cattle. I'm not telling you what to do." Buck faced the door.

"We've never given up before," Owen exclaimed.

Buck looked hopelessly at his friend. "I didn't have a family before." Buck kicked a torch aside and held his arms in the air. With a glimpse toward Owen that expressed the gratitude of a lifetime, he stepped out of the burning cabin. The smoke stung his eyes as he stumbled into fresh air. He raised his head to see Warren slam his fist into Buck's face. Buck stumbled but stayed on his feet.

"Do you think I really want to kill you?" Warren shoved his revolver into Buck's side and grabbed him by his hair. "You're strong, the strongest so far. But that's going to change. Do you know what pain really is? I'll tell you." Warren kept his revolver at the ready. "Pain is knowing your brother is dead and there wasn't a thing you could do about it! But, for you, you're going to get what I didn't. You're going to *see* yours die. And then, I'll let you live long enough to know that pain before I kill you anyway. Get movin'!" Warren shoved Buck toward the house. "Get all of them out here!"

"What about the man in the cabin?" one of the gunmen asked. Warren ignored him and watched the three remaining gunmen usher the families outside.

"Hey, there was a second son. Where is he?" a gunman asked and pointed his revolver at Beth.

The bedroom door creaked open. "I'm here. I got scared."

"Heh! Just like your father to run and hide, a coward's son."

Logan stared at the man. "My father is no coward."

The gunman thrust Logan outside with the others and grouped them in front of Warren. "This is all of them."

"Bring the oldest son here." Warren turned toward Buck and two of the gunmen. "Get him to his knees." One of the gunmen hit Buck in the head with his revolver. Buck fell to the ground. "What is it they call you? Deacon, is it? Well, Deacon, it's time to pay for the sins of your past."

Bam, bam, bam!

Everyone shuddered from the gunshots discharging from the burning cabin. Two of the gunmen surrounding the front of the cabin dropped motionless against the ground as Owen emerged from the black smoke.

Flames covered his back and legs. He fired his revolver to the last bullet, missing the remaining man by the cabin.

Bam! A single gunshot pierced the ears of the group as they looked at Warren. He lowered his aim, indicating the direction of his shot. Buck saw Owen grab his side and fall to the ground.

"Owen!"

"Shut up!" Warren aimed at Buck. "One of you go make sure he's dead. The rest of you…"

Bam, Bam, Bam!

A barrage of gunshots burst from the trees upon the gunmen. The group knelt to the ground as four more gunmen fell. The shots riddled the ground near anyone with a gun. Warren watched one of his gunmen make a stand, firing wildly into the trees. He emptied his weapon to a horrifying silence that terminated with three continuous shots that found their marks in the gunman's body. He fell backward with a hard thump against the ground.

"Warren! We're the only ones left! Let's get out of here!" the last gunman hollered from the protection of a wagon.

Warren grabbed Buck and held his revolver to Buck's head. "That's enough! Any more shooting and I'll kill him!" Warren searched the tree line. Seconds passed as a figure emerged from behind a large oak. The man approached with a brown coat and cowboy hat that shadowed his face. Warren observed the stranger stop and drop a rifle from his left hand. The last remaining gunman rushed to the stranger with his weapon drawn. "No!" Warren watched as the stranger whipped his coat to the side, exposing a holstered revolver. With blinding speed, the man drew his gun.

Bam!

The gunman fired in return, hitting the treetops in the distance. He kept running with an awkward stride toward the stranger and then stumbled a few feet before him. Everyone viewed the gunman collapse and drop his revolver near the boots of the stranger. Warren stared in disbelief as his last man went down. He cocked the hammer of his revolver. Buck thrust his elbow into Warren's throat. His weapon discharged in a violent reaction. The bullet grazed Buck's shoulder. The revolver fell from Warren's grip while he clutched his throat. Buck spun around, unaffected by the wound, and lunged into Warren. The stunned group watched the two men collide in a bruising battle. Buck thundered into Warren's ribs with repetitive punches indicative of a seasoned boxer. Warren countered with a jab into Buck's wounded shoulder. The pain registered with Buck, causing him to favor the injury. Warren's rage overwhelmed Buck's one-armed defense.

"You're dead," Warren shouted and pulled a knife from his belt. He thrust the blade toward Buck's chest.

Bam!

The knife turned abruptly and cut into Buck's side. With his uninjured arm, he smashed his fist into Warren's jaw. The loud snap of breaking bones was heard by everyone. Warren dropped the knife and fell holding his shot leg. Buck stared at the beaten man and looked to see Logan standing near him, aiming a smoking revolver at Warren. His arm began to shake with his finger teasing the trigger.

"Son," Buck whispered. "Don't."

Logan stared into Warren's eyes. A sinister expression crept upon his face. He aimed the revolver toward Warren's head. "You…"

Buck witnessed his son's manifestation and gasped at the resemblance before him. He saw himself in his son's desperation, only many years ago in his own youthfulness. The beginning of his wrath so long ago was now being witnessed in his offspring. The evil that once possessed him was now standing next to him with another revolver pointed at another soul. Buck remembered the last time he spoke with his son. "Logan, I've killed before. Don't be like me. Be better than me."

Logan's voice quivered. "They called you a coward!"

Buck's eyes welled with pride. "A coward would not have a son like you." Logan slowly faced Buck. He felt a soothing touch as Beth gently removed the weapon from his hand. Logan buried his head on his father's chest. "I love you, son."

"We need to help Owen," Beth urged.

Buck agreed and noticed the strange man still standing away from the group. "Thank you. Who are you?" The stranger ignored Buck and walked in front of Ann, revealing his identity.

Ann clasped her hands over her mouth. "Ralton!" She wrapped her arms around her brother's neck.

"This is your idea of a new life?" Ralton Jr. questioned. "You didn't say anything about this in your letter. What's going on around here?" Ralton Jr. began to choke from Ann's embrace.

"I am so glad to see you! Thank God!"

Buck assisted Owen into the house with Beth and Janet for treatment. He watched Jeb account for the wounded gunmen and then approached Ralton Jr. "Sir, thank you again. We would not have survived without your help."

"I saw the smoke and came this way," Ralton Jr. said.

"Mr. Samson, this is my brother, Ralton Hutch Junior." Ann beamed.

The two men shook hands. "That's some fine shooting you did, Mr. Hutch."

"Army training at its best." Ralton Jr. noticed Warren seated and tied to a fence post guarded by the boys. "I figured that man aiming a revolver at you warranted little explanation, along with seeing my sister in danger."

"You figured correctly. If you'll excuse me, I need to tend to our enemies, whether I like it or not." Ralton Jr. laughed while Buck nodded and approached his sons. "That's good, boys. Go see if Mr. Moore needs any help with those wounded men." He let his sons depart and then pressed his knee into Warren's bandaged thigh. "If there is any payment for sins, it will be by you. I expect you to cooperate until the authorities get here."

Warren chuckled arrogantly, ignoring the sting in his thigh. "You think you've won?" Warren laughed again. "This isn't over. You and your lady friend over there are going to feel pain. It's comin'!"

Buck grabbed Warren by his collar and thrust his head against the post. "What are you talking about?"

Warren spat in Buck's face. Buck wiped it away and pressed harder against Warren's wounded thigh.

"You fool!" Warren yelled. "Hey, woman!" Ann turned toward Warren and Buck. "I hope you said good-bye to your three children!"

"What?" Buck straightened Warren against the post.

"We saw her children leave with those buffalo. They've got a day's ride ahead of you. There's nothing you can do. When my men finish with your friend and that woman's children, they'll be back for you." Warren paused with evident anger. "Now you know what real pain feels like."

Ann stood in silent agony overhearing Warren. She instinctively turned northward in the direction of Levi, Rachel, Matthew, and Cole. Warren sneered at her with satisfaction, seconds before Buck's fist rendered him unconscious.

The sky was filled with laden clouds colored in every shade of gray. Restless winds warned of their arrival in frigid gusts. The temperature steadily declined, releasing a stinging chill upon the land. A pale hue obstructed the afternoon sunlight, casting the hint of an approaching cold front. Clouds massed on the western horizon, posing a threatening stance upon Cole and Levi.

"Rotten timing for winter to show up," Levi stated.

Cole glanced westward. "We need to hurry."

"Can the horses keep this up? We've been riding a long time." Levi observed Arrow maintaining a steady stride. Cole ignored Levi. Levi had detected Cole's reservation more than once. Curious to figure out Cole's demeanor, he continued. "I don't understand how they got so far ahead." Cole watched the ground. "Mr. Berenger, what's the matter?"

"Stop here." The two men halted their rides and dismounted. Cole walked ahead and searched the earth. "Here, look at this." Levi knelt next to Cole. "I've been watching their tracks. I can't say for sure it's them, but I count two horses and the two bison."

Levi studied the tracks. "How did they know to come this way? We haven't seen a road for miles."

"I don't know. It's almost like…"

"What?" Levi asked.

Cole returned to his horse and mounted. Levi stood in front of him in silent demand, forcing Cole to confront him. "What, you want to know? The fact is, I don't know. It doesn't seem possible that two children could come this far in this kind of weather and survive at night. It's like they're being led."

"The Wichita Mountains are right over there. They're going where they wrote they would, remember?" Levi pointed.

Cole remained unconvinced and urged his horse forward. They rode several miles watching the tracks. The cold air stiffened as the mountains grew larger. A creek twisted across the land, serving as the last obstacle before the granite foothills. Rugged cross timbers stood as the remaining threat to their expediency along the opposite bank. Levi watered the horses while Cole scanned for tracks and a passage through the forestry.

"It looks like they crossed over here," Cole said. Levi led the horses to his location. "I'm going up this rise to look." Cole negotiated a small hill and observed the terrain. "How did they know to cross here?" Cole yelled to Levi.

"My brother and sister aren't blind!" Levi jabbed. "They're obviously capable," he mumbled to himself. He led the horses farther down the bank and watched Arrow lean for another drink. Levi rubbed his companion behind the ear and looked down. His eyes widened at the sight before him. He turned to summon Cole, surprised to see him running down the hill. "What's the matter?"

"Mount up!" Cole urged. "We're being followed. There are four riders coming from the south."

"Is it Mr. Samson?"

"Their horses aren't from the ranch."

"Mr. Berenger, wait. Look." Levi pointed along the muddy bank. "Those look fresh." Both men stared at several horse tracks. "And they crossed here."

"Looks like three of them." Cole mounted and followed the tracks across the creek. He looked back at Levi with unease. "Someone is following the children."

Levi felt a surge of fear combine with the biting cold. He rushed to Arrow and dashed across the water. Cole raced through the undergrowth and powered through to the other side. The terrain opened to a natural field dotted with cedars and scrub oaks. The clearing offered a spectacular view of the massive boulders and granite features of the Wichita Mountains. The rounded peaks and rising rock slopes portrayed an array of rust and gray shades. Several boulders appeared the size of houses piled upon each other. The impenetrable rock formations rose from the earth and towered above the surrounding Great Plains. The men paused to witness their first sight of the unique display.

"We're not getting through that on horseback," Levi commented.

"I doubt anyone can." Cole looked in every direction. "We need to improve our odds." Levi gazed at Cole in confusion as he continued.

"That game preserve is farther north. I'll keep tracking the children and skirt the mountains. You ride that way and find some help." Cole pointed away from his destination.

"No, I'm going after my brother and sister," Levi countered.

Cole turned his horse next to Levi. "We don't have time for this! Ride ahead and look for anyone that can help us."

"No!" Levi yelled. "That's my family out there! I'm not leaving them to *hope* I find someone to help."

"Listen, kid, none of this is looking good for your family. I'll do what I can, but I don't want your maw standing over the graves of three of her children if I can help it!" Cole's eyes pierced through Levi's stunned expression. Without further discussion, Cole turned his horse and kicked it into a rapid departure.

Levi sat upon Arrow watching Cole ride away. His mind swirled with the moment, trying to fathom his circumstance. His curiosity about Cole and his confusion about his reserved personality revealed a weakness in his brawny nature. In his own way, Cole was protecting Ann by hoping to spare Levi. The situation appeared grim. Levi considered the unknowns. The remote location left him feeling alone and vulnerable. He stared into the Wichita Mountains and beckoned his faith. The majestic peaks and daunting granite rocks offered an unforeseen calmness. The prairie whispered to his soul with the wind, bestowing a sense of belonging. Arrow raised his head and looked back at Levi, expecting a command. Levi thought of his recent past and the struggles his family had endured. He thought of his future—ambitions, hopes, and dreams. He thought of his writing. He glanced at Cole's path in pursuit of his brother and sister. Another man's decision was again thrust upon him. A decision, just like his father's before, that left him without any say or choice. He remembered the infuriating words of his father: *Someday, you will understand.*

His fists tightened around the reins. He sat up in the saddle no longer feeling the cold December air penetrating his stamina. Along the distant ridge, the ground elevated to a sizeable foothill. "Come on, boy. We make our own decisions now." Levi turned Arrow toward the hill. Without provoking, Arrow sensed his rider's request. The stout animal dashed in a semblance of its name. Levi became one with his mount as they streaked across the field and up the grassy slope.

They reached the summit and trotted carefully around the boulders. "Wait here, boy." Levi climbed to the highest point of the hill. The view stretched in a panoramic display that could only be rivaled by the granite peaks behind him. His observation shifted to the previous direction of their pursuers. He looked toward the creek unable to see beyond the forestry. A sudden movement drew his attention near a collection of cedars. *I thought he said there were four riders*, Levi pondered, watching two horses behind the limbs.

Bam! Ping!

Levi ducked instinctively as the boulder near him chipped from the ricochet. Another shot struck near Arrow. Levi slid off the rock and bolted toward his horse. He grabbed his companion and led him down the other side of the hill. He searched the terrain below while leading Arrow through the constricting boulders. Another gunshot whizzed overhead. "Where is that coming from?"

He secured Arrow behind some larger boulders and continued to the top of the hill. He peered to the other side, noticing the two riders galloping toward him. "We're surrounded." Levi pulled his rifle from the case and hurried to locate the horsemen. *Where are they?* The sky darkened with the incoming clouds, causing visibility to deteriorate. Uncertain of his position, he adjusted for a better view.

"Drop that rifle!"

Levi didn't move. His mind surged to escape the situation before regret consumed him. He lowered his rifle and rested it against a rock.

"Turn around."

Levi shifted his stance. His attention focused upon a man standing near Arrow with a revolver at the ready.

"Henry, over here!"

A second man appeared through the boulders holding a rifle. His long, white beard draped over his chest. He angled to trap Levi between them. "There's only one?"

"Are you alone?" The first man cocked his revolver. His unbuttoned coat rubbed against Arrow, exposing a silver badge.

"Are you lawmen?" Levi asked.

"I'm Officer Quinton Carter, Wichita National Forest and Game Preserve."

"Am I on the preserve?"

"Don't get smart with me," Officer Carter warned.

"No, I don't mean to. Fact is I don't know where I am."

"What were you doing firing that rifle? Are you hunting?"

"I never fired it. Someone was shooting at me!" Levi exclaimed.

"Henry, did you see anyone else?"

"I wasn't trying to." Henry faced Levi. "Those shots didn't come from you?"

"No. I saw some riders coming from that direction, but there could be more of them." Levi took advantage of the moment. "I need your help. Those men are after my brother and sister. I can't find them, but I know what those men want. I don't have time to explain it."

"I think you had better make the time," Officer Carter suggested.

"Here!" Levi grabbed the muzzle of his rifle and held it toward Officer Carter. "Take my rifle. I'll do whatever it takes to get you to trust me."

Officer Carter reached for Levi's rifle. He took the weapon and observed Levi's desperation. "Where do you think your brother and sister are?"

"I'm not sure. I have a friend looking for them. We were tracking them over there when we split up. That's when I was fired at."

"Are they all on horseback?" Henry asked. Levi nodded. Henry then glanced at Officer Carter.

Officer Carter seemed uncertain of Levi's tale. He reluctantly acknowledged his partner. "Go ahead, Henry. Find them. We won't be far behind you. And watch your back." Henry shouldered his rifle and rushed to his horse.

"I have no idea where they are," Levi stated again.

"We'll handle that. Henry Hanks is the best tracker in Oklahoma. And he knows these mountains better than anyone."

"Officer Carter, Henry sent me to tell you that he spotted those men," a familiar voice shouted from below. "He's going to see how many there are."

"Good. Thanks, Peter. Keep your eyes open."

"Peter?" Levi looked behind Quinton and saw a young man with a rifle standing on top of a boulder.

"Levi?"

Levi ran to his brother. Peter jumped off the boulder and met him halfway. The two brothers extended their hands. They looked at each other momentarily and surrendered to a firm embrace. "What are you doing here?" Levi asked.

"I work with the game preserve. I'm training to be an officer. I even carry my own rifle when they let me!"

"I thought you had disappeared for good. Wait till Maw finds out. She'll be so happy." Levi informed Peter of the family's circumstance. His younger brother gasped at the situation, anxious to join Levi in the search for Rachel and Matthew.

Officer Carter listened to the account between the two brothers. Confident of the story's credibility, he interrupted Levi. "Our job out here is to protect the animals on this preserve. You both need to understand that we don't have the resources for an extended search for your siblings."

Levi used the officer's statement in segue. "Does that include protecting bison?"

10

"Did those men take the bait?"

"Yeah. They headed up the other side of that rise. It should buy us some time."

Terrell Severs turned his mount toward the distant hill. "Any chance you got rid of that kid? They're obviously on to us." The other rider remained silent. Terrell exhaled his disgust. "You boys are gettin' soft. When we catch up with the other four, you'd better improve your aim. Come on, before those two get wise to us."

"Terrell, those two men rode like they were the law."

"There ain't no law out here I know of. Besides, there are only two of them."

"I don't want any trouble with the law! I'm in this for the money," one of the two riders said. "We're cattle rustlers, not Warren's gunmen."

"Your money is tied up in that white buffalo we've been tracking. That thing will fetch a whole lot extra when we go back for Samson's cattle. So shut your mouth and let's go find those children," Terrell directed. "We're running out of daylight."

"Those children are getting help somehow."

"That's no matter," Terrell replied.

"What about Berenger?" The other rider asked. "If he gets in your face again, faking your name as 'Smith' won't matter. He won't hold back this time."

"Leave him to me."

The wind howled through the valley and trees. The nearly full moon began its ascent above the clouds. The veil illuminated across the sky. The temperature plummeted with the remaining daylight. Winter's first bombardment had finally arrived.

Cole fastened his collar and pushed his cowboy hat firmly on his head. He slowed his horse to a trot and continued searching the ground for tracks. The escaping light hindered his effort. He dismounted in a small clearing and knelt on the ground. Any indication of the trail was gone in the rocky terrain. Frustration amplified as hope began to sway. He grabbed the reins and walked ahead. Even with his proven experience and determination, he struggled for how to find the children. Desperation infiltrated his thoughts as he spotted a man's silhouette in the distance. Cole drew his revolver. "Who are you?" The profile remained motionless between two cedars. He fixated upon Cole without reply. Cole cocked his revolver, indicating his intention. "This is the last time I'm asking!" The figure slowly raised his right arm, motioning Cole forward. Cole watched for any indication of a weapon. The silhouette lowered his arm and walked behind a cedar. "Hey!"

Cole pulled the reins and aimed forward. He looked ahead to see the man standing on the opposite side of another small field. Cole watched the man continue walking. He mounted his horse and followed. The man disappeared through more trees. "Wait!" Cole quickened his pace. He rode around the man's location and into another opening with various sized boulders scattered near a dense forest.

"Shh! Did you hear that?" Rachel whispered.

"I can't hear anything. I'm getting cold. We need a fire. Where is he?" Matthew asked.

"He'll be back. He's taken care of us this far. Put on your extra coat." Rachel wrapped a blanket around her brother and sat with him. They cuddled between the boulders, free from the stinging wind, and finished eating some corn cakes.

"I sure miss Mrs. Samson's suppers. Aren't her biscuits and sorghum the best you've ever had? I never wanted to tell Maw, I didn't want to hurt her feelings." Matthew dreamed of previous meals.

"We'll go home soon. He said these are the mountains we're looking for." Rachel tried to remain positive for her little brother.

"This is not how I thought I would be spending *my* Christmas Eve." Both children giggled and sipped some water from their acquired canteens.

Ssscuff!

The children leaned forward and watched the outlet between the rocks. A shadowed mass moved in front of the opening. Matthew crawled from the blanket to the edge of their enclosure. He leaned forward as the wind collided with his face. He rubbed his eyes and opened them to witness a slimy, black object smear down his cheek. "Ah, Spirit! Yuck!" Matthew wiped the residue of the small bison's nose from his face. "Are you cold?" Matthew reached under Spirit's chin and rubbed. The jumpy animal calmed from Matthew's scratching and released a satisfying sneeze before Matthew could duck.

Rachel unleashed a belly laugh that echoed across the rocks. "Bless you!" Spirit mooed a low tone as if in response.

Matthew wiped his face again as the expelled congestion dried in the wind. "I feel like a booger." Rachel erupted in laughter. The two siblings enjoyed their little friend. Matthew noticed Spirit's mother standing nearby. Her dark fur camouflaged in the dimming light. "It sure is easy to see Spirit. His white hair glows like a ghost."

"Good," Rachel replied. "It will be easier to see him this time. Is his maw still out there?"

"Yeah. Should we give her a name too? We've been calling her *maw* forever."

"I don't know. Mr. Samson said if we give them all names it will be harder to say good-bye to them," Rachel said.

"Oh. Do you think we will see his paw again?"

"I don't know. I wonder if he followed us or left for good."

"Why would his paw leave? No paw would leave their…" Matthew became quiet.

"What's the matter?" Rachel tugged him, startled to see tears in his eyes. "Why are you crying?"

"Our paw left us. So maybe you're right."

Rachel felt numb. Her determination vanished with Matthew's words. She took him into her arms and cried. The many months of harbored emotion flowed between them. They embraced without concern for their situation. The longing release of their sadness and confused pain united them. They held each other with the innocence of children and with the hope of someday having reprieve.

The sound of their horses neighing gained their attention. They released from each other to see Cole standing at the entrance. The children stared at him without acknowledgement, emotionally drained for any fear of a scolding. They noticed their horses standing behind him as he held their reins. Cole witnessed their distress. They shivered in front of him. He shrouded his relief of their presence. Their tired eyes and feeble faces pierced his callous heart. A sentiment he had never felt for anyone manifested within him.

Cole removed his cowboy hat. "Your horses were looking for you." Both children lunged for Cole, hugging him tightly. He wrapped his arms around them, pulling them closer. Rachel buried her face against his chest.

Matthew clutched to his duster and exposed his tear-soaked cheeks. "I missed you, Mr. Bear Ranger."

Cole relinquished his restraint. "I missed you too." He hugged them as if they were his own. "You two are frozen. Don't you know you could die out here? There's a winter storm coming." Both children waited for Cole's admonishment that never came. "At least you picked a good spot to get out of the wind." He handed them the reins and walked into the forest. The children secured the horses and saw Cole return with his arms full of wood. He piled the pieces between the boulders and lit a fire. Dried brush fueled the flames as it roared to life. The children gathered around the soothing warmth. Cole opened his satchel and dumped several food items at their feet. They tore into the morsels savoring every bite.

"How did you find us?" Matthew asked with his mouth full. "Did our maw come too?"

"It wasn't easy trying to find you. And your maw stayed behind. Is there anyone that came with you?"

The children looked at each other before Rachel responded. "Our Indian friend came with us. He showed us where to go."

"Why?" Cole asked.

"So we could bring Spirit home. And his maw and paw, when we can find them," Matthew replied.

"Where is your friend now?"

"We don't know. He wants us to wait here," Rachel answered.

Cole realized his questions were leading to more questions. "I want you to wait here too. Get warm. You're staying here for the night. But keep the fire low. I don't want anyone to see it. I'm going to get some more wood and keep watch."

Matthew ran to Cole's side. "Don't leave us."

"You two were quick to leave before."

Matthew stared at his coat and toyed with a button. Rachel stepped from the fire and approached Cole. "Will you stay with us tonight?"

"I could think of warmer places to spend Christmas Eve, but it seems I don't have much choice. Why are you asking? You've been on your own for some time now."

"We don't like to sleep anymore." Rachel looked back at the fire.

"And why is that?"

"Because we dream," Matthew interjected.

"Everyone dreams. It's part of sleeping."

Rachel had a bizarre expression. "But our dream is the same for both of us."

A large bonfire burned with brilliance that could be seen a mile away. The flames licked the cold, blustery air in a battle of the elements. The firelight flickered in the open field and danced along the bordering cedars. The canopy of clouds glowed from the covered moonlight casting a pale hue across the landscape. Except for the bitter cold, the evening displayed everything expected of the season.

"That's them. This is where the tracks stopped before I ran out of daylight," Henry Hanks said. "They're holding up for the night."

Officer Quinton Carter observed the scene. "Looks like you were right, Levi. I see several of them bedded down around the fire. Some horses are gathered north of them." Their hidden vantage point atop the ridge provided clear observation. "Peter, you aren't going to like this, but I need you to get back to the station and alert all of the reinforcements you can. That will be challenging on Christmas Eve, but we need to let the superintendent know what's going on. Bring a wagon back with you and plenty of ammunition, water, blankets, food, and bandages just in case."

"But that's my brother and sister out there!"

"I know. But you will be helping them by helping us," Quinton encouraged.

The brothers faced each other. "I hope nothing happens to them," Peter stated.

"I know. Be careful going back," Levi paused. "Hey, I am going to see you again, right?"

"Yeah." Peter's tone changed. "Levi, I didn't mean to hurt Maw's feelings, but I needed to leave. I hope you understand that."

"I do now." The two brothers acknowledged each other without words. The shared moment passed in silent understanding and a revelation of mutual respect. Levi watched Peter mount his horse and trot away into the darkness.

"Let's move in." Quinton returned Levi's rifle to him. "I hope you won't need this, but just in case…" Levi took the rifle. They mounted their horses and rode quietly down the ridge. The firelight blinded their natural night vision as they entered the field. The red embers crackled from the heat, drawing their attention from the surroundings.

"How many horses did you see?" Henry whispered.

"Two, maybe three. It was hard to tell. They weren't standing directly in the firelight," Quinton replied.

"Wait!" Levi warned. "Something's not right." He stopped Arrow and looked around. "It's a trap."

"What?" Quinton halted his mount with Henry.

"Why build a fire in the middle of a field if you don't want to be seen?"

Quinton looked ahead. "Could it be your friend with your brother and sister then?"

"No. Mr. Berenger would know better. My other rancher friend and I saw this on a cattle drive from Vernon. Rustlers do this to lure you in and then steal your herd." Levi thought of Buck.

"Or set an ambush," Henry interjected and quickly turned his horse. "Get back to the tree line."

"Where are they going?" Terrell Severs and his six men watched Quinton, Henry and Levi hurry back to the trees.

"They're smarter than I thought," Terrell exclaimed and lowered his rifle.

"What do you want to do now?" one of the men questioned. "It's freezing out here."

"Get two men to follow them. They will go for high ground so watch that ridge. They can see the whole valley from there." Terrell looked into the darkness. "Those children have got to be bedded down around here somewhere. Whatever you do, don't let them get that white buffalo on to the preserve. If it gets into those mountains, we'll never find it. Keep a rider ready in case we see it."

"But that still doesn't help if those three come snooping around again. It's beginning to get crowded out here. It's just a buffalo, Terrell. It's not worth getting shot over."

"The white buffalo is money. I told you that! I want Berenger. Let that fire burn down and go get your things. Scatter the men along that boulder field. You can camp and share watch through the night. No one will see a fire in all of those rocks. And it's the last place we haven't looked for those children." He leaned toward the gunman with vengeful eyes. "Whether it's that buffalo or Berenger, I'm not leaving here empty-handed."

Rachel and Matthew hurried through the brush and trees nearly out of breath. They searched the area for what they knew was there, but could not find. Panic drove their pace as they ran through a maze of thick forest and fog. Neither child wanted to accept the dreaded presumption that they were lost. They continued through the trees and in to a clearing on the other side of the woods. Oaks and bushy cedars surrounded the perfect opening. Across the way, a natural granite entry cut between several huge boulders that led into the heart of the Wichita Mountains. The children observed the beauty of the area, noticing the route as the only accessible means through the rugged terrain.

A branch snapped behind them. They held their breath and turned around. An Indian man poised behind them, adorned in his native winter wear. He held a bow in his left hand and a long spear in his right. A quiver, tightly packed with crafted arrows, was strapped across his back. The wooden handle of a knife wrapped in cord and secured in a skin sheath draped from a leather strap around his waist. He stood proudly with the strength and presence of a skilled plains hunter.

The children smiled at the recognition of their friend. They felt a sense of peace in his presence. The Indian swiftly stabbed his spear into the ground. He opened his fur outer garment, revealing a circular, wooden pendant fixed to his clothing. It was decorated with interwoven strands resembling a web and a collection of small feathers dangling from the bottom. The children gazed curiously at the item, admiring its appeal. The Indian watched the children's reverence of him. Pleased with what he had come to know, he expressed a slight smile in return. He closed his garments and pointed behind the children. They looked to see the natural entryway again. Aware of the location, they both turned back to witness their Indian friend was gone.

"Wake up, wake up, Mr. Berenger!"

Cole Berenger snapped awake and pointed his revolver into Rachel's face. Rachel reeled from Cole's aggression. Cole blinked to remember his situation and realized he still held Rachel at gunpoint. "Don't ever do that again." Cole breathed heavily and lowered his weapon. The adrenaline slowed as he came to his senses. The dawn remained hidden behind the clouds, but brightened steadily along the eastern horizon. Cole felt specks of water tingle across his face. "Is it morning yet?"

"Yes, sir, almost. It's starting to snow. We need to go," Rachel insisted.

Cole noticed Matthew warming himself over the coals and coughing while he ate the remains of their food stores. "Go where?"

"We need to take Spirit home. We know where to take him now."

Cole rubbed his eyes. "And how do you know that?"

"Our Indian friend told us. Come on!"

"He was here?"

Rachel became impatient. "It's hard to explain. Please come on." Matthew coughed in the background.

"How long has your brother been coughing like that?" He grabbed his revolver and crouched by the boulders.

"I don't know, since last night maybe?" Cole pushed her gently toward the base of the boulders.

Matthew coughed a third time. "Matthew!" Cole whispered. "Cough into your coat." Cole stepped over the dying fire and peered across the boulders.

Bam!

The rock's edge shattered from the impact of a bullet near Cole's head. He jumped to the other side of the boulders and peeked between them. Two men angled toward him from the distant cedars. Cole grabbed the children and moved them to the entry. A large divot in front of the entrance captured his attention. The white dusting outlined hoof prints the size of his hand in the snow. "Whatever made those prints is huge."

Both children stared across the field. "Mr. Berenger, look!" Spirit and his mother emerged from the thickening snowfall at the edge of the woods. "We've got to help them!"

"No you don't!" Cole demanded. "Stay down." The sound of hooves impacting against the ground echoed over the rocks. They all looked to see a horseman closing on the bison and twirling a lasso above his head.

"No!" Matthew screamed. He scrambled to his feet and burst between the boulders toward Spirit.

"Matthew!" Cole aimed to their rear. One of the gunmen spotted Matthew from his position.

Bam!

Cole fired, narrowly missing the gunman. The man ducked as the second gunman took aim at Cole. He fired and hit Cole in the shoulder, knocking him against a boulder. "I got him!" The gunman yelled as he and his counterpart signaled to the tree line.

"Get down, you fools!" Terrell yelled at them from the forest. "That boy drew you out too soon!"

"There's the second one," Officer Quinton Carter spoke hastily.

"I got him," Henry Hanks acknowledged.

"Fire." Both men shot their rifles at the same time, prone beneath a cedar tree. Their two targets slammed backward onto the ground.

"Levi, go!" Quinton urged. "We've got their attention." Levi prodded Arrow and sprinted from behind a line of cedars.

"You idiots!" Terrell cursed their predicament. "Those shots came from over there."

"They didn't go to high ground! Maybe it's more men?"

Terrell became furious. "Cover our horseman!" Terrell saw Cole holding his shoulder and running toward Matthew.

The three remaining gunmen unleashed a barrage upon the cedars. Bullets ripped through the limbs and pelted the ground. Quinton and Henry took cover at the base of the trees.

"Mr. Berenger, what do we do?" Rachel ran to his side.

"Grab your brother and get into those trees over there!"

Matthew ran into the path of the oncoming horseman. The horseman kept his focus on Spirit, preparing to fling the lasso around its neck.

"Matthew, come on!" Both children came to a standstill with the horse running full stride toward them.

"Get out of the way!" the horseman yelled, noticing the children. In an instant, Cole barreled across the horse's path and tackled the children into the trees. The horseman flung his lasso, wrapping it around Spirit's neck. He secured the rope around his saddle horn and watched it tighten upon Spirit. "Whoa!" The horseman fumbled for the reins as Arrow rushed from behind the cedars.

Levi leaned against Arrow holding his rifle by the barrel. Timing his pass, he rose in the saddle and swung the rifle. *Whack!* The stock slammed into the horseman's chest. The man rolled backward off his mount. He hit the ground and bounced unconsciously into the cedars. The rope holding Spirit unraveled from the saddle horn and dropped near the children. "Rachel, grab the rope and run toward the mountains with Matthew," Levi ordered. "Mr. Berenger, can you make it?"

Bam!

A bullet zipped by Arrow. "Get out of here! I'll take care of the children," Cole replied.

"There are two Game Preserve officers over there. Go southwest and you will be on the preserve. I'll see if I can lead them away from you." Another bullet cut through the trees as Levi directed Arrow to safety.

Cole gathered the children and ran into the woods. Rachel tugged the rope still fastened around Spirit's neck. Its mother followed at a steady trot. Cole kept pressure on his wound and forced the children ahead. The ground inclined slightly leading toward the first rise of the Wichita Mountains. "Keep going that way. We can hide in the mountains and wait for help."

"But that's the wrong way," Rachel exclaimed. "We're supposed to go *that* way."

"Don't argue with me!"

"I'm sure of it! We saw it in our dream. The Indian wants us to go that way."

"Enough of your Indian friend! Do as I say. Go!" The children reluctantly pulled Spirit closer and continued up the rise. Cole slowed his approach. He felt his undershirt soaking in blood and pressed harder against his shoulder. He turned around at the sudden sound of a horse crashing through the brush behind them. "Children, get to that mountain. Go hide in the rocks and keep going as far as you can."

"Mr. Berenger, we need you."

Cole exhaled in frustration and pain. He hurt with every step to catch up to the children. He rounded some brush and saw the children with the two bison standing together. "What's the matter with you two? I told you to get to that mountain!"

Matthew pointed ahead. "We can't. Look!" Cole observed an eight-foot wire fence along the terrain. The sturdy metal structure lined the border of the preserve. Cole glanced in both directions of the fence unable to see a way through. Thick brush and trees dotted the forest, surrounding them as the bison became restless. Cole felt fatigue overcome him. He dropped his gun belt and removed his duster. He sat against a tree and winced from his wound.

"You're cornered." Cole spun around to see Terrell Severs aiming his revolver. "And it looks like one of my men hit their target," he sneered. "You children drop that rope and follow that fence out of here." Rachel and Matthew remained still, staring to the left of Terrell. "Did you hear me?" Terrell pulled the hammer back on his revolver, keeping his eyes on

Cole. He noticed the children's attention away from him. He glimpsed left in disbelief. An Indian stood in front of the second exit to the area. He towered in stature, holding his spear and bow at the ready. Terrell shifted his aim toward the Indian.

"No!" the children screamed.

Cole pulled his revolver from the leaves. "Children, run!" He fired at Terrell. The bullet passed by his head and cut through a tree limb. Terrell ducked and shot back. Cole rolled behind the tree and returned fire, covering the children as they scurried southwest with the two bison. Terrell watched the children escape and kept shooting at Cole. He looked for the Indian and heard horses at the rear. "Men, over here! I've got Berenger pinned down." Bullets erupted from behind him. Terrell panicked to see Quinton, Henry, and Peter moving to surround him. He grabbed his horse and rode through the brush.

"Matthew, come on!" Rachel yelled while keeping up with the bison. The children ran to their limit. The rope tangled in the brush causing Spirit to stumble. Matthew untied the rope from its neck and ushered him on. They ran through the forest heaving breaths of cold air.

"Where are we?" Matthew yelled.

"Just keep running."

They pushed through the obstacles and away from the fence. "I have to rest." Rachel entered a small clearing surrounded by oaks and bushy cedars and waited for Matthew. They stopped to catch their breaths while Spirit stood between them.

"Matthew, look." Rachel pointed to a large gap in the fencing. Fresh mounds of dirt around the metal posts indicated the pending construction. Ahead, a natural granite entry cut between several boulders leading into the mountains. The children recognized the formations as though they had been there before. "It's just like my dream," Rachel said.

"And mine too."

They both looked at Spirit. "You're home." Rachel rubbed under his chin.

"Do you hear that?" Matthew asked. A horse jumped over the brush bordering the clearing. Terrell flung a rope over Spirit and wrapped it around his saddle horn. He forced his mount backward and tightened the restraint. The little bison bellowed from the strangling pain, jumping and kicking to free itself. Its mother rammed the horse in defiance. The horse reared, throwing Terrell from the saddle. He landed on the ground holding his knee.

"You stupid animal!" He pulled his revolver from the holster and fired. The mother bison bawled and rolled onto her side. Terrell looked at the terrified children staring at Spirit. The fledgling white bison stepped near its motionless mother and grunted. It then released a series of calls that carried across the terrain. Terrell watched his horse free itself from the rope and run to the corner of the clearing. "Get over here!" It turned away, trying to get out of the enclosure. Terrell faced the children and stared at the Indian standing behind them. The Indian stood at the opening of the fence looking down at the female bison. Without moving his head, the Indian angled his eyes at Terrell. The children backed away from the opening as the Indian squared his stance. "You're going to need more than a bow and arrow!" Terrell threatened and aimed his revolver.

Click!

The disturbing sound led to the realization that he forgot to reload. He watched the Indian continue to stare at him and then slowly back away behind a boulder. The ground began to rumble as Terrell saw a bull bison charge from the boulders. The huge creature thundered through the opening, ripping the ground with every stride of its hooves. It lowered its enormous head, exposing its blunt horns. Terrell aimed at the beast, frantically pulling the trigger with no result. The bull bison slammed into Terrell with full momentum. Its right horn punctured his rib cage, carrying him screaming into the forest. The tree branches and dense undergrowth tore at Terrell's passing flesh. The bison stomped with a fury and tossed its head, sending Terrell airborne. The lone gunman smashed against a tree. His body fell awkwardly against the ground at the feet of Quinton and Henry.

The bison calmed and observed the gathering humans. With an instinctive display, the majestic animal lumbered back to the clearing. Terrell's horse became frenzied at the bison's return and bolted through the brush. Spirit nudged its dead mother a final time and moved slowly near the waiting bull. The two creatures stood at the opening of the fence. Spirit tossed his wet, black nose toward the children. Rachel and Matthew waved and cried at the dreaded departure. Spirit bellowed a low tone. The animals meandered between the boulders and gradually disappeared into the mountains.

Levi approached Rachel and Matthew and hugged them. The children continued crying. "I have a surprise for you." He pointed across the clearing.

"Peter!" The three of them ran to each other and embraced in a sibling's welcome. Their reunion was brief as the children observed the dead female bison.

"What are we going to do for her?" Rachel asked and wiped her cheek.

"We'll take care of it," Quinton responded. "We'll make sure she's buried properly. You can even visit the grave sometime if you want to." The children nodded with little relief. "Peter, why don't you and Levi take your brother and sister to the wagon and get reacquainted? We've got some quick work to do here. Those other gunmen fled so we'll get the reinforcements after them." Quinton addressed Rachel and Matthew again. "This is no way for children to spend Christmas Day. Give us a few minutes and then we'll all go get some food and warmth."

The family approached the wagon tired from the trek through the woods. The children noticed a man sitting on the rear gate. "Mr. Berenger!" Rachel and Matthew ran to Cole. He held them one at a time with his free arm. They observed his sling and each child hugged him again.

"And people wonder why I never had children." Cole laughed. "Did that man hurt you?"

"He tried to fight that big paw buffalo. He lost," Matthew said.

"There was another buffalo?"

"We'll get you caught up on the way. Come on, children, let Mr. Berenger rest," Levi urged.

Cole stopped the children in front of him. "I almost don't want to ask, but what possessed you to do all of this?"

"All of what?" Matthew asked.

"To drive two bison across country in the winter to these mountains?"

"We did like the Abernathy boys," Rachel replied.

"The who?" Cole asked wearily.

"From Mr. Samson's story…the Abernathy boys from Frederick, Oklahoma. He told their story about when they went to New York all by themselves. So Matthew and I thought we could do it, too, but just to the mountains to take Spirit home. I guess we didn't go by ourselves the whole way like they did. Our Indian friend did help us a lot. Do you think we will see him again?"

"I don't know. I don't even know what you're talking about. But I do know that when we get home, I'm going to punch your *Mr. Samson* right in the mouth."

The children climbed into the wagon and sat on each side of Cole. Levi joined Peter and watched the moment unfold with Cole and the children. Matthew looked at Cole while he witnessed his tired eyes. "I wish you were my paw." Rachel smiled at her brother's statement. Matthew leaned next to him and faded asleep. Cole placed his good arm around Rachel as she snuggled against him and closed her eyes.

The wagon started forward in a bustle of noise muffling Cole's response. "Me too."

11

The wind swept down the plains with invigorating waves of warmth. Field flowers and redbuds decorated the rolling countryside. The rich green backdrop highlighted the vibrant white, yellow, and purple colors scattered across the landscape. Crisp new leaves of every tree glistened in the sunlight. Birds sang their anxious greetings and celebrated the awaited transition. The previous evening rains had washed away the remnants of hibernation and satisfied the young season's thirst. New life flourished throughout the land in a joyous welcome to another springtime in southwest Oklahoma.

Fresh lumber was stacked between two small houses. Construction of the first home was complete. Work on the second house was following suit with the completion of the interior walls remaining. Sturdy roofs and solid walls provided freedom from the weather and treasured nights of sheltered slumber in real beds. Nearby, the rich soil experienced the plow for the first time, lined in fields of pampering effort. The lined sprouts of future harvests had already taken root. Cattle grazed the area in expanded herds intermingled with more horses. New fencing sectioned the land with proud borders as a testament to the accomplishments developing within. The untamed land known as the Big Pasture to those before was now an expansive sight of farming, ranching, and living in 1911 Oklahoma.

"Ralton, at the rate you're going, you could have your own town by year's end," Buck teased.

"It's coming along. We should have a decent-sized barn finished by the end of spring. I can't thank you enough for the help. It would have been another year before we started the second house."

"That's what we do as neighbors and family," Buck responded and shook Ralton Jr.'s hand. "And thank you for the fine meal today. Your lovely wife sure can cook." Several horses and wagons surrounded the first house. The Samson, Rowe, Hutch, and Moore families massed at the front of the home with Cole and Owen.

Buck called Levi from the crowd gathered around him. "Folks, I'm going to borrow this young man for just a moment." Buck walked Levi toward the tree line within sight of his grandparents' graves. "I need to talk with you before you go. There never seemed to be a right time and I didn't want you to leave and not know."

"Sure," Levi answered.

"You know I told your maw about the man that murdered your grandfather. His real name was Severs, not Smith." Levi nodded. "I didn't tell you at the time I found out because I didn't want you burdened with it. I didn't want you tempted with revenge. That's a path you never want to follow. You and your family had already been through so much and I didn't see how telling you that would have helped any."

"Mr. Samson, you and your family are the reason were are even here. Without you, we would not have made it. Thank you for always caring for us. I know it got hard at times. I'm going to miss you a lot." Levi extended his hand.

"We're all very proud of you." Buck wrapped his arms around Levi. "You're a good young man. I know you will do well."

"Thanks for your talks with me. I won't forget that cattle drive from Vernon. And I'm glad you and Logan talked. Your sons are blessed to have you as their father. I know I would be. And take care of Arrow for me. I love that horse." Buck and Levi walked back to the waiting families. Levi gathered his belongings and piled them into the Moore family's wagon. He gave his farewells and gratitude, saving his family for last. Ann waited patiently for her turn. They embraced with tears of a son's endearment and a mother's love.

Ann held Levi at length. "My son is going to be a college student. Go get your dream. I'm proud of you."

"I'll miss you, Maw. I'll write often. Norman is not that far away. I'll come home every chance I get. I love you." He kissed Ann on her cheek and faced Peter. "Thanks for coming. I wasn't sure if the Game Preserve would let you go."

"Cole helped a lot in capturing those remaining men. With all that mess done, it made it easier to be here," Peter explained.

"Maw is very proud of you. We all are. Don't stop until you become an officer. Hope things go well for you."

"Yeah, you too." The two brothers hugged. Levi watched Peter join Ann and then he quickly reached into the wagon. He placed an object wrapped in burlap on the ground in front of Rachel and Matthew.

He fought back his tears, unable to contain the emotion choking his words. "I won't be gone long. I promise." The children's eyes welled. Levi grabbed his sister and brother in a firm embrace. They held each other in a lasting moment engulfed with memories and love. "Here, I have something for both of you." Levi unwrapped the burlap covering and revealed a leather journal. "I'm going to college to be a writer. And this is the first story I have written. I wrote it in Maw-Maw's journal. It's a story about our journey to Oklahoma, everything we did together here and your adventure taking Spirit to the Wichita Mountains." Levi handed it to them.

Rachel opened it to the first page. "The Dream Catcher," she read aloud. "Is this about our Indian friend too?"

"Well, sort of. I wasn't sure how to explain your Indian friend from what you told me. If he shows up again, you can tell him about it. But, it's your story. It's our family's history in Oklahoma. I want you both to read it before you go to bed each night. That way, you will know that I will be thinking about you and that I love you both very much." They hugged again. "And when I come home to visit, you can tell me what you thought about the story." Sadness was replaced with excitement. Rachel and Matthew took turns holding the journal, fighting over who would read it first. Levi embraced Ann a final time and bid farewell to his aunt, uncle, cousins, Cole, and Owen. He climbed into the wagon and waved.

Jeb Moore secured his family in the wagon with Levi. "Don't worry, Ms. Rowe. We'll get this boy of yours to Elgin and then on his way to Norman." Ann thanked him for Levi's transportation. Jeb snapped the reins and they galloped away with Levi waving until they were out of sight.

"Mr. Bear Ranger, look what my brother gave us!" Matthew ran to Cole. "And look, your name is in it too." Ann joined them to see the journal.

"That's one story I don't have to read," Cole stated.

"Why?" Rachel asked.

"Because thanks to you two, I already know how it ends!" Cole grabbed the children and tickled them. They giggled and ran to the creek. "Ms. Rowe, I don't know how you keep your strength with those two. But you certainly have raised them well. They're fine children."

"Thank you, Mr. Berenger. I know they think the world of you. And I never got the opportunity to thank you again for your sacrifice for them. You saved them. Levi said it could have been much worse had you not gotten involved."

"I just wanted to help." Cole tipped his cowboy hat and departed.

"Mr. Berenger."

Cole turned around.

"I don't mean to be sudden, but if you would like to join us for dinner tonight, I know the children would enjoy it. It would help ease them with Levi's absence."

Cole beamed with fervor. "Yes, ma'am. That would be nice. Thank you. And if you would, you can call me Cole."

She smiled. "And I'm Ann. We'll look forward to seeing you tonight, Cole."

Cole tipped his hat a second time and bumped into Owen. "That's an awfully big grin you've got sprawled across your face there, cowboy."

Cole's smile disappeared. "Shut up." He walked away with Owen snickering behind him.

"Ms. Rowe, are you going to be all right?" Buck asked with Ralton Jr. walking next to him.

"I'm fine. I got to see the day that two of my boys became men. And I have my family back." She held her brother's arm with pride.

"Where are those two little cyclones at?"

"They ran off to the creek with their journal. You'll probably hear them fighting over it," she replied. "Ralton, did you ever bury that skeleton by the creek? I don't want the kids around that again."

"I never saw it," Ralton Jr. responded. "I looked all around that area you showed me. The bones must have washed downstream."

"I hope so. We don't need any more excitement around here for a long time."

"Buck, why don't you all join us for dinner?" Ralton Jr. asked. "We have plenty to finish from lunch. It will just be my crew, Ann, Peter, and the children."

"You all go ahead without us. We are going to have dinner as a family tonight," Ann said.

"That's a lot of food for just the four of you," Ralton Jr. exclaimed.

Ann hesitated. "Mr. Berenger is joining us too. It will make the children happy."

Ralton Jr. raised his eyebrows. "I see. As long as the children are happy, what more could we ask for?"

"Shut up." Ann's face flushed as she left for the house.

"So much for not having any more excitement around here," Buck mocked as he and Ralton Jr. laughed at Ann's hasty departure.

Rachel and Matthew ran through the woods and up the creek bank. "It's over here, I know it."

"Maw will skin you good if you get near it again," Rachel warned.

"It's just a skeleton." The children searched the creek bank for the bones. Unable to find them, they returned to their first location. "This is the spot. Maybe the bones got buried again."

"Let's go read the story." Rachel led Matthew into the trees along the creek and leaned against a large cottonwood. She opened the journal with Matthew by her side. "The Dream Catcher, by Levi Rowe," she read aloud. "Chapter one."

"Rachel, look." Matthew pointed into the limbs hanging in front of them. The children stared at two objects tossing in the wind. They removed the items from the branches.

"They're dream catchers," Rachel exclaimed. "They look just like the one our Indian friend wears." They studied the circular crafts, admiring the netting and soft feathers dangling along the bottoms of the circles.

"Maybe he made them for us?" Matthew wondered.

"I don't know."

The wind intensified through the creek bed, churning the leaves and foliage. The children turned around, startled at the pages of the journal flipping furiously in the strong breeze. Rachel ran to the journal and placed her hand on the turning pages to keep it from blowing away. Matthew joined her as she picked up the journal, bookmarking the pages with her hand.

"Did Levi draw that?" Matthew asked and pointed at the page. Rachel moved her hand, displaying the sketch of a dream catcher. "It looks just like ours." They held their dream catchers next to the drawing. Each web design and feather was a precise match. "How did he know?" Rachel closed the journal. She tucked it under her arm and held her dream catcher next to Matthew's. Eager to show off their finds, they ran up the slope and hurried to their new home.

Epilogue

"Kids, don't wander too far. Stay where we can see you. We will be heading back to the car soon."

"We will, mom," Kaitlyn responded and darted after her little brother. "Nathan, you had better come back or mom will get mad."

"Kaitlyn, come over here quick!"

She hurried through the cedars and stopped by her brother along a small clearing. She watched several bison grazing on the winter grass. "There's so many of them." The bison herd passed calmly in front of them, strolling among the cedars.

"Kaitlyn and Nathan! What did I tell you?" their mother scolded as their father stood nearby. "Those bison are dangerous. They could have charged you!"

The father walked next to his children and whispered, "They're pretty neat, aren't they?"

The children teemed with enthusiasm. "Yeah! They got really close to us, but they didn't bother us," Kaitlyn stated.

"I know that was exciting, but don't get that close again, okay? Mommy is right. Hiking the Wichita Mountains is fun, but the animals on the refuge are wild and they can be dangerous."

"Those buffwoes are big, daddy! They're as big as our car!" Nathan said. "I wish Great-Grandpa Matthew could have seen them."

Their father smiled at their eagerness and the memory of his grandfather. "I'm sure at one time, he did. Come on, little hikers. Let's go this way." The parents walked through the cedars with the children in pursuit.

"Nathan, wait! Look over there. There's another one." They stopped as their parents continued and watched a female bison eating along the edge of the clearing.

"What's that?" Nathan pointed. Both children watched as a baby bison stepped from behind its mother.

"Aw! It's so cute," Kaitlyn said.

"Are baby buffwoes supposed to be white like that?" Nathan asked. Before his sister could answer, they watched a man step from the foliage behind the two bison. "Who is that?" The three observed each other in silence. The man stared at them without expression and then slowly raised his hand with a slight smile. The children smiled in return.

"Kids, don't make me come back over there!"

The children reluctantly backed away and hurried toward their parents. "He looked nice," Nathan said and kept running. "What kind of clothes was he wearing?"

"I don't know," Kaitlyn replied. "But his dream catcher looked just like ours."

CPSIA information can be obtained
at www.ICGtesting.com
Printed in the USA
LVOW04s0851140916
504482LV00002B/2/P